# THE WOLF'S WOUNDED OMEGA

A.J. CANE

The Wolf's Wounded Omega

Copyright © 2024 by A.J. Cane

All rights reserved.

All rights reserved worldwide.



Cover Design © Cormar Creations

Editing: Jersey Devil Editing

Oops detection: Anne Victory Editing

# PROLOGUE – FOUR MONTHS AGO

*DANNY*

I closed the front door as quietly as possible, wincing when the latch clicked into place. The sound might be almost imperceptible to a human, but if Rex was awake, he'd hear it clear as day, and that was the last thing I wanted.

"Where have you been?"

I froze, my heart hammering like crazy. "W-work."

"I don't believe you." The words were practically a growl.

I turned slowly, searching the dimly lit open-plan living area for my boyfriend. If I were calmer, I'd be able to hear the thud of his heartbeat and the rasp of his breath, but as it was, everything was drowned out by the pounding of my own pulse.

There he was. Leaning against the kitchen counter, his arms crossed over his burly chest, his eyes narrowed. He pushed off the counter and stalked toward me, and I fought the urge to back away. When Rex was in a mood like this, it never ended well, but making it obvious I was afraid of him only aggravated him more.

"Tell me where you were," he demanded, towering over me.

"I f-finished at the bakery and then c-came home," I stammered.

He leaned close, sniffed, and shook his head. "I can smell other alphas on you. Have you been sleeping around on me again?"

"N-no." My voice wavered. "I've never cheated on you. I promise. I stopped at the police station on the way and talked to Zander."

He stiffened. "Why did you need to talk to Zander?"

"He's my brother." And he was also in charge of the local police force, so I could understand Rex's concern. If Zander—or any of my brothers—discovered the truth of our relationship, Rex would be in deep trouble.

He shoved me against the wall, moving so quickly I didn't have time to react. The breath rushed from my lungs and I gasped, desperate for air.

"Zander isn't the only alpha I smell on you," he snarled.

I cowered, unsure how to convince him of my fidelity. He kept me pinned there with one hand. Then, all of a sudden, his other hand cracked across my face.

I stared at him, stunned, as my cheek burned. Tears sprang to my eyes.

He'd hit me.

Sure, it wasn't the first time, but usually he released me immediately after, the guilt clear in his expression.

Not now.

His eyes glittered gold, his bear coming to the surface. They gleamed with fury as he grabbed me beneath my armpits and lifted me off the ground.

I considered lashing out with my legs. Even though omegas were weaker than alphas, I was larger than average and could probably land a solid kick to distract him. But perhaps he just wanted to frighten me, and once he realized he'd achieved that, he'd put me down again.

Unfortunately, that wasn't how it went.

Instead, he slammed me back against the wall. A sharp pain flared in my side and I cried out.

"Shut up!" He dropped me, and I slid to the ground, clutching my ribs. "Who is it? One of the policemen? Tell me his name."

"There's no one," I croaked.

He manhandled me until I fell onto my side and then he drove his foot into my solar plexus. I curled up, shielding myself with my legs and arms.

He kicked me again and again. Despite my enhanced healing capacity, the blows ached, and I was afraid he might rupture something vital.

When he struck my temple, stars exploded on the insides of my eyelids.

Fuck.

He wasn't going to stop.

I grabbed for his leg, holding onto the ankle so he couldn't kick me again. He swung something at me and knocked me off. Gritting my teeth, I allowed a partial shift to ripple through me and slashed at him with my claws. The coppery tang of blood filled my nostrils and he swore.

"You fucking—"

I swiped at him again, and he moved backward, giving me enough room to scurry away. I considered shifting fully, but it would be easier to get out the door in this form. I lunged toward it, reaching for the handle, pain lancing through me everywhere Rex had struck me.

Claws circled my ankles and he pulled me back. I smacked face-first onto the ground and my ears rang. I tried to focus, to fight, but my mind was fuzzy.

A noise outside caught my attention... or had I imagined it?

I called out, cutting off abruptly when Rex clapped his hand—now clawless—over my mouth and straddled me. He held me still, and I no longer had the energy to struggle.

He was older. An alpha. If he wanted to hurt me—even kill me—there was only so much I could do to protect myself. I hadn't been trained to fight like my brothers had. I was a pastry chef. A baker. I liked to create sweet cakes that made people happy. I didn't know how to fend off an angry alpha bear.

But just as I internally admitted defeat, a roar sounded on the other side of the door, and with an almighty crash, it splintered inward.

A massive grizzly charged through the ruined doorway and tore Rex off me. The bear tossed him across the room and, when Rex dared to rise, smacked him back down. The bear leaped on Rex, pinning him to the ground. I wondered briefly if Rex might shift, but as I dragged myself around to see what was happening, he remained in human form.

Perhaps he realized that he stood no chance against Everett, whether he was a bear or a man.

The grizzly shrank, his fur receding and bones readjusting themselves until my naked brother appeared atop Rex.

He looked over at me. "Are you okay?"

"Yeah." It was all I could bring myself to say. I wanted to squeeze my eyes shut, curl into the fetal position, and pretend none of this was happening.

I couldn't believe he was here. As much as I was grateful to him for saving me, it was beginning to sink in that he knew the truth now. He knew how weak I was, and what I'd allowed to happen.

Everett stood and ground his foot onto the center of

Rex's back. "Pack your shit and get out. You have two minutes."

He backed away but kept his eyes on Rex as he scrambled up and bolted for the hall. Neither of us moved or spoke as we listened to him stuff things into a backpack in the bedroom. Less than a minute later, the back door slammed, and he was gone.

"Stay away from Grizzly Ridge," Everett shouted after him.

We both knew he'd hear and that he'd see it as the order it was. Everett might not be the Clan Alpha or even the second-in-command, but he was an enforcer, and Rex would be a fool to disobey a direct order from him. While Rex might be paranoid and cruel, he wasn't stupid.

Everett padded over and dropped to his haunches beside me. "Fuck, Danny. What did he do to you?"

I pressed my lips together to stop myself from crying.

"Hey, now." He touched my shoulder gently. "Come on. Let me take you to Momma."

Panic tore through me. "No!"

If Momma saw me like this, then Dad would too, and before long, the entire family would know what a failure I was. Shame churned in my gut and burned up the back of my throat.

No one would look at me the same after this.

CHAPTER

# ONE

**D**ANNY

As the clan gathered in front of the wooded area behind my parents' house, the most intriguing scent hit my nostrils: a mixture of pine and leather that was strangely enticing. I breathed it in and looked around, searching for the source.

I weaved between the clan members that were hovering near the food table nibbling on the finger food that Momma had prepared, and moved toward the house. As I did so, the combination of pine and leather grew stronger, but I couldn't quite figure out where it was coming from.

Before I could track it down, Dad's voice boomed through the yard. I pushed into my tiptoes and spotted Milo and Everett a few feet away, so I made my way to them, listening as Dad told the clan about Milo's kidnapping yesterday and his safe return.

I was tempted to cling to Milo. I'd felt sick when I'd seen him getting taken away, and I'd worried myself into such a state I was surprised I didn't have an ulcer. I hadn't known him for long, but he was impossible not to like. There was something so sweet and guileless about him.

Once he'd finished giving a rundown of the confrontation at Moonlight Cove, Dad announced Milo's pregnancy. His pride was evident in the warm gaze that landed on Milo and the subtle expansion of his chest.

I ruffled Milo's hair. If anyone deserved happiness, it was him.

"We also have a new clan member," Dad continued. A figure moved behind him. "I'd like to introduce Knox Kingston."

The new clan member came into focus as he stepped up beside my father. A breeze stirred my hair, and my gut dropped as the scent I'd been following intensified. Knox's dark gaze swept the gathering, stopping when it locked on me. His eyes flashed from brown to green, and his fangs dropped. He took another step forward.

My chest seized.

Oh, fuck. Fuck, fuck, fuck.

The scent was him.

And the fact I could smell him like this and was reacting so strongly could only mean one thing: he was my fated mate.

I stumbled backward, horrified as my own fangs dropped, responding to him.

No, no, no.

This couldn't have happened at a worse time. I was broken. Scared of alphas. What if I disappointed him?

What if he was like Rex?

I spun away from him and started running, tearing off my clothes as people sprang aside to let me pass. As soon as I was naked, I shifted and fled into the woods, crashing through the underbrush, too unnerved to pay attention to where I was going.

I ran and ran until my legs were shaking beneath me,

but no matter how far I went, that intriguing scent of leather and pine followed me. I couldn't outrun it.

Eventually, I slowed and perked my ears up. Thankfully, no one seemed to be on my tail. I slumped against a tree, grateful to my fur for keeping me warm and protecting me from the roughness of the bark.

I closed my eyes and my mate's image appeared in my mind. Gods, he'd been handsome. So tall and broad, looking like a sexy badass in his leather jacket with his dark hair tied at the nape of his neck. His full lips had parted when he'd seen me, and I couldn't help but imagine how plush they'd feel against mine.

Not that I'd ever find out. I was too fucked up for that.

All I could focus on was the fact he was several inches taller than me and that his hands were twice the size of mine. He could do some real damage with those things.

And he was a former mercenary.

I may not have seen him before tonight, but my brothers had mentioned the alpha wolf who'd been involved with kidnapping Milo. Surely, someone capable of hurting an omega as sweet as Milo couldn't be trusted.

Although... he had changed allegiances when he'd scented his mate on Milo's clothing.

His mate.

*Me.*

No. I couldn't think about that.

I dragged myself back to my feet and looked around, not a hundred percent sure which direction I'd come from. In my distress, I hadn't taken the time to get my bearings or pay attention to the sights and scents I'd passed along the way.

I took off in the direction I thought led back to my parents' house. Once I was moving again, my thoughts returned to Knox. The alpha fated to be mine. Was he upset? He'd probably imagined meeting an eager little omega who'd be happy to merge their lives straight away.

Instead, he'd gotten me.

The gods weren't smiling on him today. I wasn't as small as most alphas wanted or as docile, and as I'd already proven, I had some issues.

Assuming Knox wasn't an evil, kidnapping psychopath, he must be so disappointed.

A familiar scent tickled my nostrils, and I paused. It wasn't the tempting aroma of my mate, or the comforting smell of my family and Grizzly Ridge. It was something darker that reminded me of one of the most terrible nights of my life.

Bitter coffee. Rex's scent.

My gut lurched, and I stopped immediately, pivoting to go in the other direction. I had to get away. I had to—

I bowled into a grizzly that had been approaching me from behind. The bear stumbled backward, catching himself before he fell.

Oh gods, he'd found me.

I sprinted away, moving as quickly as my furry legs would carry me. But as I dodged a tree, a voice called after me.

It wasn't Rex. It was Zander.

I collapsed to the ground and allowed myself to shift back to my human form. "It's Rex," I panted. "I smelled him."

Zander rushed over and dropped to his knees beside me. He was naked, like me, but it didn't bother either of us. Shifters were accustomed to seeing each other without clothes on.

"It's just his cottage." He started to reach for me, but then stopped. "We're almost on his land."

A growl rumbled through the woods, raising the hair on the backs of my arms.

That wasn't Zander.

My brother grabbed my arm. "Hurry. There's been enough fighting this week. We need to get out of here."

# TWO

K NOX

I approached Everett and Milo with my heart in my throat. "Hey."

"What?" Everett growled, obviously pissed at the interruption to their impromptu make-out session. I didn't care. There were more pressing things to worry about.

I tugged the end of my ponytail, my gut clenching as I tried to give voice to my fears. "My mate…" I began. "Did he just reject me?"

Sighing, Everett released Milo and turned toward me. "I wouldn't say that."

I kept my eyes firmly on him, ignoring the red patches of beard burn on Milo's face. "Then what was it?" Because it sure as hell felt like rejection. He'd seen me and run off into the woods to escape. "I thought when I met my mate, they'd want me as much as I wanted them."

I'd never expected this. I'd risked my professional reputation, turning on my employer to help Milo because I'd known he'd lead me to the person who was meant for me. Now I couldn't help wondering if the gods were playing a sick joke on me. Hadn't I experienced enough rejection without my mate abandoning me too?

Everett grimaced. "The bear who ran away, you're sure he's your mate?"

My eyes narrowed. "Yes. Why?"

Was he already spoken for? Dating?

My chest constricted.

"He's my little brother," Everett said.

"Oh." I wouldn't have guessed that. "He's much hotter than you."

Everett grumbled, and Milo snuggled against his side. My heart ached. That was what I wanted. An omega to call my own. Someone who would always want me around. A man I could make a life with.

"Danny, my brother, was in a bad relationship recently."

*Danny.*

What a sweet name for a gorgeous person.

"I won't tell you more than that," Everett continued. "You'll have to ask him yourself. But the point is, he's wary of getting hurt again, so you'll have to be patient with him."

Wait. Hurt? What kind of hurt?

I gritted my teeth. I hated to imagine my Danny in any form of pain, but if he'd been abused, then I'd hunt down the guy responsible and make him pay.

"I'll be as patient as it takes," I promised.

But only with Danny. Anyone who touched him without using the utmost care deserved whatever they got.

"Good, because if you mess with him, I'll tear you apart."

I smirked. I'd like to see him try. "Understood."

I offered him my hand. We hadn't gotten off on the best foot, but if he was going to be part of my family, I'd better try to fix that. He gripped my hand firmly and shook. As soon as we broke apart, he gathered Milo close.

I moved away to give them privacy, ignoring the slight twinge when I recalled the fact that I'd hoped to end my night that same way, with my own mate in my arms.

I backed up against the side of the house and leaned on the wall, gazing into the woods. Somewhere out there, Danny was roaming in his bear form. Should I have followed him? His family had stopped me, but being separated from him felt wrong down to my bones.

Gods, I hoped this wasn't the beginning of another massive rejection.

Surely it was bad enough that I'd been exiled from my pack's homeland because my father had seen me as a threat rather than a son—never mind that I hadn't given him any reason to think I wanted to take his place as Pack Alpha. Fate wouldn't be cruel enough to give me a mate that didn't want me.

Would it?

I wasn't as certain of the answer as I wanted to be.

I watched as more of the clan members stripped off their clothes, shifted, and made their way into the woods.

My wolf itched beneath my skin, fighting to come to the surface, but I flexed my hands and breathed deeply, keeping him inside. If I let him out, he wouldn't have the same restraint as me. He'd hunt down our mate, and if we frightened him, I'd never forgive myself.

Instead, I looked around at the few people who remained in the area. Everett and Milo were still plastered against each other. The Clan Alpha, Aaron—my mate's father—was speaking with his wife, Melinda, on the deck. A slim figure was seated on a picnic chair on the ground at the end of the deck. I wandered toward them.

As I drew near, I used my wolf's eyes to see more clearly.

The figure had dark, silky hair and was reading something on his phone screen. I inhaled the earthy, herbal scent that I generally associated with healers.

"Hi," I said, drawing closer. "Can I sit?"

He gestured at the ground beside him. "If you don't mind the dirt. I brought a chair because I've learned it's best to be prepared. I don't run as hot as you shifters do."

I lowered myself to the ground and crossed my legs, ignoring the cold that seeped through my jeans. "You're a witch?"

He nodded. "I'm Li. You're Knox, right? Danny's mate."

"If he's willing to give me a chance." That was a very big "if" at the moment.

Li switched off his phone screen and angled himself toward me. "Danny is a really nice guy. Fun. Loyal. And he makes the best honey-glazed fruit pastries in town. He'll come around, as long as you don't push him."

"I hope so." I stared into the dark, noting movement between the trees. I couldn't smell Danny though, not strongly enough to imagine that one of the figures might be him. Wherever he was, he'd gone far enough away to dilute his scent.

"You're new to town, right?" Li asked.

"Yeah." So new that I didn't even know where I was going to sleep tonight.

"Have you got somewhere to stay?" he asked, as if reading my mind.

"Not yet." I hated to admit it. It felt like yet another way in which I was a failure. I couldn't provide a comfortable home for my mate.

Li patted my shoulder, and I flinched, caught off guard by the sudden contact. He withdrew his hand. "Sorry. I'm used to being touchy. Most shifters are very physical."

"It's fine." Back when I'd been part of a pack, I'd been

used to casual affection too. Now, people rarely touched me except in violence. That was a consequence of the job I'd chosen.

"My mate Yuri's parents own a small home on the edge of town that they've been meaning to renovate so they can rent it out as a vacation home." Li nibbled on his lower lip. "It's a bit rough, but it's livable, if you'd like to use it."

Something loosened in my chest. "I'd be happy to work on it while I'm there."

I wasn't taking a handout.

He looked dubious. "Do you know much about renovation?"

I shrugged. "Enough to get by. I can paint, sand, measure, hammer nails. If they give me instructions, I should be able to muddle through."

He brightened. "That would be great. They're out on the run at the moment, but we can talk to them when they get back."

"Thank you." I wasn't quite sure how to respond. I wasn't used to people going out of their way to help me.

Li returned his focus to his phone screen and I sat quietly beside him. I closed my eyes, picturing the look of horror on Danny's face before he'd spun and stumbled into the woods.

There was a tug on my heart, almost as if an invisible tether was drawing me toward him.

Someone had scared him.

Sure, tonight he'd been afraid of me. Maybe. But only because of what someone else had done to him.

If I ever found out who had terrified my mate like that, I'd wipe them off the face of the earth.

CHAPTER

# THREE

*ANNY*
*I ran as fast as I could, my legs pumping, muscles burning, lungs screaming for air, but it was useless. Rex caught me easily, sinking his claws into my calves and dragging me back onto the land he'd claimed.*

*I looked around for Zander, but he'd vanished. No one was here except for Rex and me.*

*He tossed me through the open door into the cabin he'd taken ownership of and barreled in behind me, shutting the door and locking it.*

*A chill ran through me.*

*"P-Please don't..." I trailed off. He'd never given me mercy before, so why would he now?*

*A metal rail appeared above his bed. He hoisted me up with one arm and suddenly a cuff materialized around my wrist, connecting me to the bar.*

*My chest seized. I struggled to draw in a breath but couldn't. I jerked my arm, and metal clanged against metal. There was no way to get out.*

*No way to escape.*

I bolted upright, panting heavily.

"Darling." Fingers brushed my shoulder and I flinched away. "Shh. It's all right. Momma's here."

I blinked, my sleep-blurred vision clearing.

I was in my bed. At home. Safe.

"Where's Zander?" I asked, needing to be sure all was well.

Momma sat on the edge of the bed, her hand resting on my leg. "Probably getting ready for work. What's this about?"

I exhaled shakily and forced myself to concentrate. It had been a nightmare. Of course. Last night, we'd gotten clear of Rex's land without any problems. He hadn't confronted us, presumably too cowardly to go head-to-head with my oldest brother.

"Just a bad dream." I tried to smile, but the expression was tremulous.

"Oh, darling." Her face creased, sympathy shining in her warm brown eyes. "Are you okay?"

"I'm fine." I ignored the fact that I'd been a blubbering mess when Zander brought me home last night, and that he'd had to put me to bed like a child.

Momma arched her brow. "Fine, huh?" She tsked. "I've made pancakes with honey. Why don't you shower off your nightmare and join me for breakfast?"

"Here?" I asked. There was every chance she meant back at her place, and I didn't feel like facing anyone else yet.

"Yes."

I wriggled deeper beneath the blankets. "But it's so cozy in bed."

"Honey pancakes," she reminded me.

"Fine," I huffed. "I'll be out soon."

I waited for her to leave the room and then hurried to the bathroom. I showered quickly, dried myself, and dressed in dark jeans and a T-shirt. It was a work day, so no sweatpants for me. Fortunately, I wasn't working the opening shift this morning, so I didn't have to be at the bakery at the crack of dawn.

The rich scent of coffee wafted down the hall, and I followed it to the open-plan living area, where Momma sat at the table, one hand beside a plate stacked high with pancakes. Another plate waited opposite, along with a steaming mug of coffee. I pulled out the chair and joined her.

"Don't worry, I sweetened your coffee," she said.

I wrapped my hands around it, enjoying the warmth, and raised the mug to my lips to sip. "Perfect. Thank you."

The creases at the corners of her eyes deepened. "You're welcome. Now, tell Momma what's going on."

I squirmed. I should have known better than to think I could get away with dismissing my nightmare without further discussion.

"It's nothing." I kept my gaze off her, cutting into my pancakes, slicing them into bite-sized pieces and stuffing one into my mouth. Mm. Deliciously fluffy and sweet.

I felt her eyes on me but didn't look up.

She sighed. "You know, you and I were the only omegas in our family for a long time. While I haven't been in your shoes, I think I have some idea of how you're feeling."

I mumbled something indistinguishable and munched more pancakes.

"People put too much emphasis on secondary gender roles," she continued. "Just because alphas are bigger than us and stronger than us, that doesn't mean we're weak."

This time, I did raise my eyes. She wasn't eating, just staring at me levelly.

"We are, compared to them," I pointed out.

She cocked her head. "Do you consider Milo to be weak?"

"Of course not!" Milo had survived so much. He deserved to be recognized for that.

Momma smeared one of her pancakes with liquid honey. "He was kidnapped and didn't manage to escape on his own."

"But he did what he needed to protect himself and his baby." Irritation heated my gut. I didn't know where she was going with this, but I wouldn't stand for her denigrating my new brother.

"It still happened." She raised her fork, then paused. "You're saying you don't think he's weak?"

"No." I forked the pancakes with more force than necessary.

She ate too, remaining quiet for an uncomfortably long time. When she finally did speak, she caught me completely off guard.

"If Milo isn't weak, then you aren't either. No"—she held up her hand—"let me finish. As omegas, our power comes from our clan. We inspire their loyalty. We give the alphas something to protect. We draw everyone together and keep the clan whole and healthy. Just because we aren't as physically powerful as them, that doesn't mean we aren't strong in our own way."

I drank more coffee, weighing her words. I understood where she was coming from, but I'd grown up as the youngest of four brothers, and the only omega. It was difficult not to directly compare myself to them.

I was the smallest.

The only one who hadn't been trained to fight.

I was a baker, while my brothers dedicated their lives to protecting our hometown and those within it.

"Tell me more about my mate." I couldn't give Momma the response she wanted now, so it was best not to give her any. Hopefully, this would distract her enough to forget what we'd been talking about and honestly, I did want to know more about Knox.

She reached for her glass of orange juice, the silence dragging on until I wondered whether she might not let me get away with the change of subject. Fortunately, she must have realized how much I needed her to.

"I don't know much more than you." She drank, keeping her gaze on me. "He's an alpha wolf shifter. A paid mercenary. My understanding is that he stays on the move and picks up jobs as he goes."

I frowned. If he was constantly on the road, did that mean he wouldn't want to settle in Grizzly Ridge? Because I couldn't fathom leaving.

Not that he probably wanted me after the scene I'd made last night.

"Any questions you have, you should ask him directly." Her tone was gentle but chiding.

I groaned. "Are you here to badger me into talking to him?"

She pursed her lips. "I'm here to check on my son because last night was hard on him."

I shrank in my chair. "Sorry, Momma. I know that."

My mouth moved faster than my brain sometimes. It was one of the things that had created problems between Rex and me. He hadn't wanted a sassy omega. He'd wanted a sweet one.

"Darn right, you did." She nodded reprovingly. "That said, I do think you should give yourself a chance."

"Myself?" I asked before I could think better of it.

"Yes." She pushed her plate away, apparently done. "To discover that you're strong enough to stand beside an alpha like Knox."

The back of my throat tightened and tears sprang to my

eyes. It was as if she'd looked into my heart and seen my deepest fears.

"I'm not," I whispered. "Especially so soon after Rex. I'm... I'm broken."

No one could possibly want a mate like me.

# FOUR

**K**NOX

My paws hardly made a sound as I raced across the damp earth, winding between trees and sparse bushes that had lost most of their leaves already. A familiar scent called out to me, and I stopped so quickly that my back legs skidded and I nearly lost my footing.

My mate.

I doubled back, searching for the source of the delicious sugar-and-honey scent that belonged to Danny. As it grew stronger, I noticed a sharp metallic undercurrent—that of an omega in distress.

I stiffened. Was Danny out here? Was he hurt?

Moving faster, I encountered the origin of the scent trail, and halted once again. The trail was at least a couple of days old. Danny hadn't been here recently.

In fact, looking around, I realized it was possible this was where he'd run to get away from me after leaving his parents' home. We were only a couple of miles from the back of their property.

My heart sank as I scuffed my muzzle along the dirt,

doing my best to breathe in as much of him as possible. If the trail was from then, it meant that the distress he'd been experiencing was because of me. I hated knowing that I'd caused my mate any kind of discomfort.

I straightened and followed the trail, curious to see where it would lead. Another scent joined Danny's and I growled.

An alpha.

My growl deepened. Whoever they were, I would rip their throat out. Danny was mine.

But almost as soon as it had gathered, my tension dissipated. I recognized the alpha's scent. It was one of Danny's brothers. The cop. I had nothing to fear from him.

I continued to follow the trail until it forked—in one direction, heading toward his parents' house, and in the other... Well, I'd just have to find out.

I trotted along, my nose low to the ground to make sure I didn't lose the scent. Not that I was likely to. It was the most intoxicating thing my sensitive nose had ever smelled.

A few hundred yards away, I arrived outside a large house. Based on its location, it must be on the same road as the one the Alpha lives on. But then I thought I heard Milo say that all of the family live along the same street. I scanned the area but didn't see anyone, so I padded closer. My mate's scent was pooled around the house. This must be his home.

I sat back on my haunches. He had a nice place. Better than what I could offer him. The cabin Li and Yuri had taken me to, after speaking with Yuri's parents, was habitable, but that was about the most that could be said for it.

Damn.

I shook my head. No, I should be pleased that my mate was comfortable. It was ridiculous to be unhappy that I hadn't been the one to provide for him.

I turned away from the house and resumed my run around the perimeter of the township. All the while, my mind was consumed by thoughts of Danny. The dark waves of his hair. The deep brown of his eyes, which had become golden as his bear surfaced.

Stunning.

When I returned to the cabin I was now renting, I shifted on the front doorstep and collected the key from underneath a loose board. I unlocked the door and let myself in.

Inside, the cabin was somehow even colder. The walls seemed to preserve the chill. Shivering, I wandered naked through the small living area to the bathroom. I took a quick shower and dried myself before any water was able to cool my skin further.

That done, I went to the tiny bedroom and opened my suitcase, searching through for one of my nicer sets of clothes. I tugged on a pair of dark jeans, a long-sleeved black shirt, and my leather jacket. I left my hair hanging around my shoulders. I hoped it wouldn't freeze once I left the house.

I considered riding my motorcycle to the bakery but decided to walk instead. Perhaps I'd look less intimidating to Danny without the massive metal beast accompanying me. Hopefully he wouldn't be as afraid of me as he had been the other night. Surely he knew that if I'd intended to force my presence upon him, I would have done so by now.

If he didn't want me at his place of work, then I'd leave. Well, at least I would as soon as I got my coffee. There was none at the cabin and I was severely under-caffeinated.

I locked the cabin behind myself and strode up the road. The concrete sidewalk began a few blocks ahead. I shoved my hands into my jacket pockets and looked up at the sky.

It was gray and I wouldn't be surprised if it started to rain before long.

It took me fifteen minutes to reach the center of town. Even though it was early, the bakery was already bustling. I peered through large glass windows at a line of people at least six deep and reached for the door handle. I yanked it open and flinched, startled by the ding of an analog doorbell.

A couple of people in the line turned toward me but most of them didn't seem too curious. I joined the back of the line and scanned the insides of the display cabinets. As a wolf, my tastes ran more to savory foods than sweet, but the occasional treat didn't go amiss.

I breathed in and beneath the scent of pastry, cookies, and coffee, I smelled something even sweeter. My mouth watered. I may not love sweet food, but I wanted to take a bite out of whatever was responsible for that scent. Although I suspected I knew what—or who—it was.

Danny.

I craned my neck to look around the people in front of me. There he was. Behind the counter, shifting fruit pastries from a cooking tray into the cabinet. He glanced up and our eyes met. His eyes widened and he took a step back, his muscles tensing and his scent souring with a hint of fear.

My stomach dropped. He was still scared of me.

I held up my hands to show I meant no harm. "I'm only here for coffee."

At that, everyone who'd previously ignored me turned toward me.

"J-Just coffee?" Danny stammered.

"That's all, I promise."

I waited to see what he'd do. There was every chance he'd ask me to leave, and if he did, I'd respect that. I wouldn't want to, but my mate's comfort came first.

"Okay then." He nibbled on his lower lip, his hand shaking as he finished unloading the pastries. Once he'd finished that, he raised his gaze to mine. "What type of coffee would you like?"

One of the men in line ahead of me grunted in protest, but Danny ignored him.

"Espresso," I said. "Double-shot."

Danny's mouth twisted in a little smirk. "You do seem like the type."

What did that mean? Was it a compliment... or not?

I didn't ask, and he turned away and began preparing my drink at the coffee machine. I watched his movements. While I'd been told that he was a baker, he clearly knew how to make a decent cup of coffee as well. He directed the espresso shots into a cardboard take-out cup and offered it to me.

"On me," he said. "Consider it a thank-you for saving Milo, and a welcome to town. Will you be staying?"

I accepted the cup and nodded. "For a while, at least."

"Okay."

Was he glad to hear it? It was impossible to tell. Last time I'd seen him, his expression had been easy to read, but now he was masking his feelings. At least I could no longer smell his fear or distress.

I held up the cup as if making a toast. "Thank you, Danny. I'll see you around."

I whistled to myself as I left, a smile creeping across my face. That hadn't gone terribly. He hadn't run away, nor had he rejected me. Things were looking up. If I could get a job, I might even call this a good day.

Sipping my coffee, savoring the rich bittersweetness on my tongue, I made my way to the police station. Considering my experience, I hoped that they might be open to employing me, at least on a trial basis.

Unfortunately, my optimism didn't last for long. Zander, the police chief, was polite and friendly but made it clear that he wouldn't be offering me any kind of job until things were settled between Danny and me. He didn't want to do anything that might upset his brother.

I understood, but how was I supposed to win his brother over if I didn't have a way to support myself in the meantime? I had some savings but not enough to last more than a couple of months.

Undeterred, I wandered from one business to the next, asking about job openings. Everywhere, it was the same. Even though no one came straight out and said it, I got the impression that they didn't think I was worthy of their beautiful omega, so they weren't willing to help.

By the time I traipsed down the path to my new cabin and unlocked the door, I was deflated. I flopped onto the sofa and rubbed the knot of scar tissue on my chest. Shifters didn't easily scar, but my father's claws had been tipped with silver when he'd tried to tear my heart out.

I gritted my teeth at the reminder that one of the people who was supposed to love me unconditionally had tried to kill me. Even though he hadn't succeeded in removing my heart from my chest, the poison still should have finished me off. The only reason it hadn't was because of a kindly warlock who'd kept me alive long enough to find a healer and remove the toxin.

I closed my eyes. I'd escaped. I was still alive. But I couldn't shake the feeling that there must be something wrong with me. If my father hadn't loved me, why did I think my mate would be any different?

# FIVE

*ANNY*

I leaned against the arm of the couch and stared at the photo I'd sneakily taken of Knox on my phone as the alpha had walked away from the bakery yesterday morning.

There was no denying it. The man was sexy.

Even from the poor-quality photo, his appeal was obvious. He gave out the type of misunderstood bad-boy vibes that used to be like catnip to me. After Rex, I was more cautious, but I wasn't blind or stupid. With that long, dark hair, a shadow of stubble on his sharp jaw, and hands half again as big as mine, he was fine as fuck.

Under different circumstances, I'd have wanted to climb him like a tree.

Unfortunately, we were living in the real world, where I had very real hang-ups about alphas. Big, intimidating ones, in particular.

I huffed and ignored the droning of *The Great British Bake Off* show in the background.

Gods damn Rex Mindle. Because of him, I couldn't even enjoy the glorious sight of my mate without an undercurrent of fear ruining it for me. I hadn't had the chance to breathe him in and revel in his pine-and-leather scent. Anytime he came near me, I was too tense to enjoy his proximity.

I zoomed in on the photo, wishing I'd sprung for a better phone so the image wouldn't be so pixelated. I couldn't remember the exact shape of his silhouette, and it was bothering me more than I'd have expected.

Perhaps I could stake out the cabin he'd rented just to remind myself.

No.

That would be the kind of thing a crazy person did. I hadn't sunk that low yet. Although if I didn't at least find a way to visually soak him in sometime in the near future, it could happen.

I exited the photo and brought up the number that Dad had given me so I could contact Knox if I wanted to. I eyeballed the digits until my vision began to blur. Blinking rapidly, I looked away, spots dancing in front of my eyes.

I opened the messaging app and started a new thread with Knox's number at the top. Nerves squirmed in my gut and I gnawed on my thumbnail, uncertain of what to do. If I messaged him, then he'd have my number, and the ball would be out of my court.

That both appealed to me and terrified me. I didn't want this much pressure falling on my shoulders, but I wasn't sure what he'd do if I gave him a way to contact me.

Hesitantly, I tapped out a brief message, then deleted it.

No, I shouldn't.

But he was my mate. I burned to know more about him. The universe has matched us for a reason. I knew I should trust in fate, but that was easier said than done.

I tried again, and cleared the second message. Eventually, I kept it simple and hit send without giving myself the time to second-guess my decision.

**Danny:** *Hi Knox. This is Danny.*

The reply came almost immediately, as if Knox had been waiting to hear from me.

**Knox:** *Hey. Glad you messaged. How are you?*

The knot in my gut eased. Okay, I'd gotten in touch with him, and nothing terrible happened.

**Danny:** *Fine. Just winding down before bed. I have an early start tomorrow.*

**Knox:** *Baking?*

**Danny:** *Exactly. I'll be preparing the bread and pastries for the morning rush.*

**Knox:** *Do you enjoy that?*

**Danny:** *Love it. Although I wish it didn't have to happen before sunrise.*

Waking early was the only part of my job that bothered me. Well, that and when asshole alphas harassed the staff. The bakery was run almost entirely by omegas, and considering our secondary gender and the fact we enjoyed baking and cooking, some alphas thought we were only there while on the lookout for a partner to provide for.

**Knox:** *I used to be a soldier. We always had to get up early too.*

Huh. I hadn't realized that about him, although I guess it fit with the mercenary thing.

**Danny:** *How long did you serve?*

**Knox:** *Only two years, then my mom died and I had to return home.*

**Danny:** *I'm sorry. Were you close?*

**Knox:** *Not exactly, but I was closer to her than my father.*

Something about the way he said that didn't invite further questioning. I racked my mind for something safe to ask, that would continue our conversation without delving into subject matter that neither of us would be comfortable with.

**Danny:** *What's your favorite food?*

**Knox:** *Venison. What's yours?*

I should have guessed that. Deer were natural prey for wolves.

**Danny:** *I love anything sweet, but especially if it includes fruit and honey. Chocolate is good too. So are cookies. Momma makes the best cookies.*

**Knox:** *Hopefully I'll get to try them one day.*

I swallowed, and my heart hammered. How was I supposed to respond to that?

**Knox:** *That wasn't me trying to rush or force anything. How did you get into baking?*

I let out a relieved breath.

**Danny:** *Actually, I'm a pastry chef, not a baker. Similar, but different. I grew up learning to bake from Momma since we're the only omegas in the family and none of the others were interested. I always knew I wanted to work with food, but I kind of lucked into an apprenticeship.*

**Knox:** *I'm sure it wasn't just luck.*

My insides warmed.

**Danny:** *Perhaps not, but luck played a role.*

For a moment, I almost asked how he became a mercenary, but thought better of it at the last minute. Wolves were pack animals. He'd said that he'd returned home when his mother died, and for him to have left his pack, something must have happened. Whatever it was, I doubted it was good.

**Knox:** *If your baking is anything like your coffee, you earned it.*

I bit my lip. I felt like he was being kinder to me than I deserved. I hadn't officially rejected him, but it must feel that way to him, yet he was being sweet and not pushing me. I'd set a boundary—even if it had been done poorly and without any kind of verbalization—and he was abiding by it.

**Danny:** *Thank you. I appreciate what you're doing.*

I meant it. From our brief conversation, I liked Knox—especially the way he was respecting my space. He hadn't turned up unexpectedly even though I knew his wolf must want to, and he hadn't made any sexual overtures when many alphas would have.

**Knox:** *What? Replying?*

I snorted, unsure whether he was trying to be funny or not. I debated whether to send him something honest but overly emotional and decided not to. Instead, I asked about the favorite place he'd traveled.

We chatted for a while longer. Eventually, I shifted to the bed and strained to focus on our messages until the last remnants of wakefulness fled.

I dreamed of being held in Knox's muscular arms, pressed against the warm skin of his chest. I turned toward him, eager to explore his naked body, but as I did so, his features morphed.

Suddenly, it wasn't Knox holding me, but Rex. His grip tightened, crushing me. Pain crashed through me.

I screamed.

# CHAPTER
# SIX

**K**NOX

The gray light of dawn cast long shadows as I turned away from Danny's house and padded into the woods. I shouldn't have come. It wasn't right to watch over him this way. Sure, we'd been messaging each other for a week now, but we hadn't spoken in person since that morning in the bakery, and he'd given no indication he wanted that to change.

I should be keeping a respectful distance, not running a perimeter check around his house every morning to make sure he was safe. What if he smelled me? I was adept at concealing my tracks, but shifters had enhanced senses. One day, he might notice that I'd been nearby.

Keeping low to the ground, I circled around the outside of the Grizzly Ridge township, searching for anything that didn't belong. That was the second part of my new daily routine. Once I'd established that all was right with Danny, I double-checked the safety of his hometown as a whole.

This morning, my breath fogged in the cold air as I moved but I didn't come across any unfamiliar scents or traces of magic. I couldn't see magic, but I could usually sense if it had been used recently.

As I reached the side of town farthest from Danny's house, my hackles went up. Something was out of place. I paused, scanning my surroundings. Nothing looked amiss, and I didn't have the restless, prickling sensation that would accompany magic usage, so it must be something more mundane.

I weaved between the trees and my ears pricked up. As I rounded a particularly thick tree trunk, a small cabin came into view. Belly to the ground, I watched it for movement.

Nothing stirred.

I nudged the ground with my nose and sniffed, then stiffened. I sniffed again. I recognized those scents. I'd become familiar with them while I was in Moonlight Cove, assisting the rogue wolf Tomas with his ill-conceived kidnapping attempt.

Wriggling closer, I drew as much of the scent as possible into my lungs. They were recent, but not too recent. Likely several hours old. Had the wolves been out here in the dead of night?

I stayed there, motionless, and counted off the minutes. Thanks to my military training, I was used to remaining still and bored for long periods of time without fidgeting.

There wasn't so much as a rustle inside, and eventually, I decided that the wolves probably weren't here anymore. With a quick look around to check for threats, I emerged into the small clearing and approached the front door.

It stood ajar. I pressed myself against the wall beside it and stayed as silent as possible. When there was no reaction from anyone inside, I nudged the door farther open. The latch was still in place, but the wood around it had shattered. They must have broken the door to gain entry.

I edged inside, the tension leaving me when I confirmed

that the one-room cabin was empty. Bunk beds lined the side wall, with a kitchen counter on the other, and considering how cold it was, the door must have been open for a while.

The pantry stood ajar. I nosed my way inside. It was empty, but the scent of dried packaged food was strong enough that I knew the pantry had recently been full. The wolves that had broken in must have stolen the food.

I hesitated, wondering what to do. In most cases, I wouldn't worry too much about someone who'd broken into an apparently unoccupied place to steal food. Most likely, they were hungry and they hadn't really hurt anyone. But the rogue wolf pack could be dangerous, and I had a mate to think about now.

With a wolfy grimace, I paced back out of the cabin and hurried toward town. I couldn't afford to let this go unnoticed in case the wolves' presence posed a threat to Danny.

I went straight to the police station. As soon as I entered, I crossed to the reception desk and changed forms. I knew from prior visits that the receptionist was a shifter and wouldn't be bothered by my nudity.

"There's been a break-in at a cabin just outside of town," I told her. "Nobody hurt, as far as I can tell, but they emptied the pantry and possibly took a few other things."

The receptionist nodded, her upper lip curled at the corner. Perhaps she hadn't forgiven me for barging past her when Milo had been kidnapped.

"I'll tell the sheriff. He just got in. Wait here. He'll probably have questions."

She stood and disappeared down the corridor. When she reemerged, Zander was on her tail, his country boy hat firmly in place despite the early hour.

"You found a cabin that has been broken into?" Zander asked, his craggy face creased as he raised his eyebrows.

"Yeah. I can take you there, if you like. Although it'll have to be on foot. I'm not sure how to get there by road."

Zander gestured toward the wall, and when I turned, I noticed a large-scale map of Grizzly Ridge and the surrounding area taped in place. "Would you be able to show me on there?"

I studied the map, noting the major landmarks. My time in the army had taught me many skills, including the ability to read maps.

"I couldn't give you the exact location, but it's around here," I said, indicating an area with the tip of my finger.

"Probably the Hadlow place," he mused, rubbing his neatly shaved chin. "I'll drive us there, and if I've got it wrong, then you can lead me to the actual site on foot."

I nodded. "If we're staying in our human skins, is there any chance you could loan me a pair of pants?"

Shifters might not mind nudity, but I didn't want my balls rubbing all over the seats of his police cruiser. Gods only knew what else might have touched them.

Five minutes later, clad in borrowed sweatpants and a Grizzly Ridge Sheriff's Department T-shirt, I sat in the passenger seat of Zander's cruiser as he drove out of town and turned onto a narrow, winding road that turned to gravel partway along. The trees were familiar, so I assumed he'd been right in his guess as to the site of the break-in.

I leaned against the door and gazed out the windshield. "I recognized some of the scents."

Zander didn't look at me. "From where?"

"My time in Moonlight Cove."

Out of the corner of my eye, I saw his jaw tighten.

"Wolves?" he asked.

"Yeah."

"Damn. Are you certain?"

I waved my hand back and forth. "The scents were definitely familiar. I'm ninety percent sure they belong to the rogue wolf pack, but they could also have been other wolves from Moonlight Cove, if there are lone wolves who live there."

He pulled up outside the cabin and stopped the car. "This is it?"

I grunted in the affirmative.

"Thought so." He paused, tapping on the steering wheel. "I'll send a deputy to look around Moonlight Cove. Real casual-like."

"Tell them to be careful." I didn't want any harm coming to someone Danny might care about.

"Will do." Zander grabbed the door handle and started to pull it, but then paused. "Have you had any luck with Danny yet?"

I pressed my lips together, reluctant to answer. "We've talked some, but if it's all the same to you, I won't say any more than that. If Danny hasn't mentioned it to you, then I'm not going to air his laundry. He deserves privacy."

CHAPTER

# SEVEN

*D*ANNY

A little over two weeks after I first messaged Knox, I stepped out of the bakery, locked the front door, and froze when movement flashed in my peripheral vision. My heart rate doubled and I remained in place, turning my head painfully slowly toward the movement, dreading what I might find.

I peered through the darkness of the rapidly descending night. Rain pelted down, hammering on the awning above, and it was difficult to see anything despite my enhanced vision. I dropped my hands from the lock, pocketed the key, and pivoted.

Then I spotted it.

Across the street, lingering in the shadows between two buildings, was a large grizzly bear.

Usually, that wouldn't be cause for concern. Grizzly Ridge was full of bear shifters. But there was something about the way this one watched me that set off all the alarm bells in my mind.

I took a step closer and narrowed my eyes. The bear

looked familiar, but it took far too long for me to realize why.

It was Rex.

I stumbled backward, tripping over my own feet. I would have fallen, if not for my back hitting the bakery window. The bear stalked forward, its massive shoulders rolling as it moved its weight from one paw to the other.

Fuck.

I briefly considered shifting, but by the time I'd made the transition, Rex might have reached me. Instead, I took off, sprinting into the rain and pounding along the street toward my parents' house.

I was instantly drenched. I shoved my hair back off my face and struggled to keep my eyes on the road ahead. Water streamed down my forehead, almost blinding me.

I panted, unused to running so quickly in my human form. It wasn't far from the bakery to Momma and Dad's house—less than a mile—but I wasn't sure if I could maintain this pace, and the slap of footfalls on the pavement behind me warned that Rex was gaining on me.

Something tugged at my chest. A crazy instinct to veer to the left and allow the soul-deep mate connection to lead me to Knox rather than going to my parents. By force of will alone, I ignored it.

I trusted my parents. I wasn't sure if I could trust Knox.

The sensation strengthened, until there was a physical ache in my chest. My bear was screaming for me to seek out our alpha mate for protection. The problem was, we weren't mated. Despite our text conversations, Knox wasn't my alpha, or my mate. We were slowly getting to know each other, but we were a long way from that.

Even though it physically hurt, I powered on, shouting Dad's name and knowing he'd come running.

I flew around the corner, onto the street where my

family lived. The turn slowed me down, and I strained my ears. But with the blood rushing through my head, I couldn't tell how close behind Rex was.

Ahead, a bear roared. Even larger than Rex, it appeared from behind the veil of rain and charged toward me. As the bear drew level, I threw myself behind him, letting my father shield me, relying on him to protect me because I couldn't protect myself.

Weak.

I bent low and used my arms to cover my head, expecting to hear the smack of flesh against flesh, but it didn't come.

I stayed tucked in on myself until a gentle hand landed on my shoulder. I flinched away and looked up into Momma's eyes.

"It's okay," she said. "Stand up, Danny. He's not here."

"He's not?" I straightened from a crouch and turned around. Behind me, Dad was pacing back and forth across the street, still in his furry form, but there was no sign of Rex.

Dad threw his head back and roared. A moment later, answering roars sounded nearby, and three hulking figures barreled down the road toward us.

My brothers.

They reached us within seconds and, upon realizing there was no immediate threat, shifted. Dad remained in his bear form.

"What happened?" Everett demanded, looking from Dad to me and Momma.

"I... I..." I couldn't even manage to draw in a full breath, let alone explain.

Momma squeezed my shoulder, bunching the sodden fabric. "Go on. You've got this."

I forced myself to inhale slowly and did my best to

loosen my tight throat. "I saw Rex. Outside the bakery. He chased me."

A growl tore from Everett. "That fucker. I should have killed him when I had the chance."

Zander grimaced. "Please don't say that when I'm around."

"Let's go after him," Garrick said, taking charge while Dad was unable to speak. "We'll track him. Momma, take Danny inside and get him dry and warm. Dad will stand guard."

Dad nodded his huge head.

Momma's arm looped around my back, and she urged me toward the house as my brothers allowed their bears to surface and they ambled down the road in the direction of the bakery. Dad stalked behind us, almost unnervingly silent.

When we reached the house, he adopted a defensive pose on the front porch while Momma escorted me in. Footsteps raced down the hall and Milo appeared in front of me. He opened his arms and I stepped into them, pressing myself against the swell of his pregnant belly.

"Are you okay?" he asked, trembling from head to toe. "I couldn't hear anything, but Aaron said you were in trouble. I would have come, but Momma told me to stay here."

"I'm okay," I promised. "She was right to tell you to stay. You need to keep my niece or nephew safe."

Milo drew back and studied my face. "I'll get you a change of clothes." He looked down at himself. "Me, too. Momma, would you like…?"

"I'll get my own," Momma replied, then opened the linen closet, pulled out three towels and handed us one each, keeping one for herself and using it to wring the water from her hair.

I stripped out of my clothes, left them in the hamper in

the bathroom, and toweled off. By the time I was dry, Milo had returned with sweatpants, a T-shirt, and an oversized hoodie for me to change into. I pulled them on and borrowed a thick pair of socks, then made my way to the kitchen, where I could hear Momma moving around.

Now wearing jeans and a knit sweater, she stood in front of the kitchen counter, her damp hair loose down her back. "I'm making hot chocolate."

"Thank you." A warm, sweet drink sounded wonderful right about now.

"Cookies?" Milo asked, emerging from the walk-in pantry with a plastic container clasped between his hands.

I was about to refuse, but my stomach gurgled, reminding me that lunch had been several hours ago. "Yes, please."

He offered me a honey cookie. I demolished it in a couple of bites. Momma poured hot chocolate into three mugs and added marshmallows to the top, followed by a sprinkle of cocoa powder. She passed one to me and one to Milo, taking the last one for herself.

"Momma said Rex came after you," Milo said as he took a sip.

I stiffened as the memory of those slapping footfalls on the pavement flickered through my mind. "He did."

But how long had he actually chased me?

He hadn't been behind me when Dad arrived. Even if Rex had been retreating by then, Dad would have chased him.

"I feel a bit silly," I admitted, blowing on the surface of the hot liquid and testing to see whether it was cool enough to drink. It wasn't too bad. "He was probably just trying to frighten me. He might not have even followed me more than a couple of hundred yards."

"You have every right to be scared."

I jumped, caught off guard by the voice behind me. I turned and found Dad standing in the kitchen doorway with a towel wrapped around his hips.

"He chased you until you were two blocks from here," Garrick called from behind him. "We tracked him back as far as the main street, but his scent vanished. He must have shifted and used his car to get away. He probably knew we'd be coming after him."

My stomach churned, and the sweetness of marshmallow and milk on my tongue became bitter.

Rex had chased me. Almost the whole way here.

What would have happened if he'd caught me? And what would he do now? Would he try again?

CHAPTER

# EIGHT

K*NOX*

Two days later, I was at the grocery store when the tinkle of breaking glass put my senses on high alert. It wasn't until the scream that I dropped my basket in the center of the aisle and bolted out of the shop.

I'd recognize that voice anywhere, even though I'd only heard it a handful of times.

Danny.

I rushed toward the bakery. It came into view just in time for me to witness a car reverse through the front window and peel away.

A breeze carried the vehicle's scent toward me and I paused for a few seconds. It was just long enough to confirm they'd been wolf shifters, and that at least one of them had been involved in the break-in at the cabin.

Danny stumbled through the broken window and shifted, his torn clothes falling to the ground as he sprinted toward the woods. Even from a distance, the sharp tang of his terror filled my nostrils.

Lurching into motion, I ran after him. He bumped into a

45

car, then tripped and almost knocked himself out on a lamppost. Panic was making him clumsy.

"Danny!" I yelled, uncertain how close to get. We'd been chatting by text message a couple of times a week, but we hadn't yet spoken much in person and I didn't want to frighten him more than he already was.

He spun toward me, stared for two long seconds, and then raced away.

"Damn." I yanked off my jacket and shirt, shimmied my jeans and underwear down, kicked off my shoes and socks, and shifted. Leaving my clothes in a discarded pile, I took off after Danny. He might be fast, but I was willing to bet that I was faster.

I caught up to him less than a hundred yards into the woods. Circling around him, I kept a wary eye on him. Mate or not, scared shifters were dangerous. Even omegas.

He growled at me and stepped forward. I kept my posture unthreatening. He took another step forward. My blood thrummed through my veins. I could take Danny on if I needed to, but I really didn't want to hurt him, and I had a feeling he'd regret injuring me too.

Taking a chance, I allowed a shift to ripple over me, returning me to my two-legged form.

"It's me," I said, holding my hands up, palms out, to show I didn't mean any harm. "It's just me. You're safe. I won't let anything happen to you."

He cocked his head, and I took a brief moment to appreciate him. I hadn't seen him up close as a bear before. He was gorgeous. His eyes were large and golden. His fur was a rich brown and looked soft to the touch.

"You're beautiful," I murmured, surprising myself. I wasn't the kind of guy who called other men beautiful. Or at least, I hadn't been before I met him. "Will you shift back for me, Danny?"

I breathed slowly, calming my heart rate and doing my best to put him at ease. Quiet settled between us, and then his body began to change, shrinking and losing all the hair except for the thick thatch on the top of his head and a patch around his cock.

I looked away instantly. Now wasn't the time to steal glances at him.

"Thank you," I said when he stood before me, naked and trembling. He dropped into a squat and wrapped his arms around his legs, rocking back and forth. His gaze was centered somewhere in the distance, and he didn't react at all as I came closer and knelt beside him.

"Everything will be all right." I reached out, and when he didn't pull away, I rested my hand on his upper back. His skin was warm, although it was rapidly cooling. I shuffled closer and encircled him with my arms, holding him close.

He remained stiff. The position was awkward, but I didn't know what else to do. His vacant stare and distracted rocking made me think he might not be completely aware of what was going on.

"Danny?" I resisted the urge to kiss his cheek. Without consent, that wouldn't be right. He was in a compromised state. Even holding him like this was tiptoeing close to the boundary. If it wasn't for the cold weather, I'd probably force myself to keep more of a distance, but I couldn't bear for him to experience more discomfort than necessary.

"Danny, you have to focus." I tried to sound stern but honestly, I was scared, and it showed. "What happened?"

No response.

"Did someone drive through your front window?"

He continued to rock.

Damn. We wouldn't get anywhere like this. I was going to have to move him and see if we could work out what had happened, either after he'd come around or based on what other people had seen.

I shifted position, scooped him into my arms, and straightened, cradling him against my chest. He was heavy for an omega, with lean muscles and a couple of inches more height than usual, but he was nothing my shifter strength couldn't handle.

I held him close, both loving his closeness and disappointed that the first time I'd gotten to touch him naked was under these conditions. It felt like we'd lost something. Still, this was what he needed.

At least, I hoped it was.

I didn't know what I'd do if he thought I'd taken advantage of the situation when he came around.

I carried him back toward town, heading for the street his family lived on rather than the bakery. Surely Zander or his deputies were already on the scene. They could speak to Danny later. They wouldn't get anything useful out of him now, and he needed comfort, not questioning.

Ahead of me, a tall, male form appeared. I breathed in, placing the scent as Everett's.

"What happened?" he demanded, rushing over to me.

"Someone drove through the bakery window and he panicked," I explained. "I'm taking him home."

"Thanks. I'll stay with him and make sure he's all right."

"Can I stay too?" It grated that I had to ask. Danny was my mate. But we weren't bonded and I had no right to sit by his side. "Please."

CHAPTER

# NINE

D**ANNY**

Reality returned to me slowly. I was surrounded by warmth, a soft mattress cushioning my body, and cozy blankets making me sleepy and restful. I blinked, and my vision slowly cleared. I was on my side, and someone was sitting on one of the chairs from the dining table beside my bed.

"Everett?" I rasped, my throat drier than I expected.

"Hey, Danny." He wrung his hands. "How are you?"

"Tired." With an effort, I repositioned myself so I could see his face. His lips were pressed together, his dark eyes serious. "Why are you... in my bedroom?"

Everett sighed. "Do you remember what happened?"

What did he mean?

Furrowing my brow, I racked my mind, searching my most recent memories. Immediately, I stiffened as images flashed through my mind in a terrifying montage.

"The window broke," I murmured, sifting through the images, trying to make sense of them. "I smelled wolves, and I ran. One of them chased me."

"We think it was the rogue wolves from Moonlight

49

Cove." Everett rubbed his bearded jaw. "They smashed through the bakery's front window and then drove away. Knox heard it happen and saw you run into the woods, so he followed you and brought you back. It was probably him you sensed behind you."

"Oh." My cheeks heated. I should have recognized his scent, but I'd been too panicked. "How did I get here?"

Everett cocked his head. "Knox got you to shift back and carried you. He's waiting in the living room. Do you want to see him?"

I flopped against my pillow as I considered the question. My mind was still fuzzy, and my muscles ached. I felt wrung out. But Knox had helped me. It wasn't right for me to continue to ignore his presence except for our text exchange. It was time for me to face him.

"Yes, please."

Everett hesitated. "Are you sure? I can tell him to come back later."

I shook my head. "Now is good."

Before I talked myself out of it.

Everett left, and less than a minute later, Knox appeared in the doorframe. He dithered, obviously uncertain whether or not to come in.

I gestured at the unoccupied chair. "Sit."

He strode over, and my heart rate lifted. There was something sexy about his long-legged swagger.

"Thanks for helping me," I said, hating the stiltedness of my tone.

Knox's dark eyes softened. "I'd hardly leave you in the woods in the state you were in." He looked poised to say more, but held back. "Are you hurt? You didn't seem it, but not all injuries can be seen from the outside."

"I'm fine." I relaxed slightly, grateful he wasn't going to push anything. "A little achy, but that's probably just from being so tense. It'll go away soon." Considering how fast shifters healed, it was likely mental as much as anything else.

"Good." He shifted his weight. "How was your day before a bunch of wolves drove through your storefront?"

I snorted, then blinked, surprised at myself for finding amusement in something that had scared me so badly. "Same as usual. I was making myself a coffee for my break when... when it happened."

"How do you like your coffee?"

Gods, he was letting me off easy.

"Full of sugar." I smirked. "I have a caramel latte with cream on top."

His mouth curved, the full lower lip thinning as it did so. "Sounds about right."

I rolled my eyes. "It's better than your bitter, sludgy double-shot espresso."

Knox's lips parted, and he huffed a laugh. Heat unfurled in my gut at how deliciously husky it was. "I'm glad you're feeling good enough to tease me."

I jolted, caught off guard. I *had* been teasing him. A few weeks ago, I'd have been too scared to do that. Perhaps I was making progress, even if it was painfully slow.

Knox stood. "I should go."

An instant denial tore through me. I didn't want him to leave. The instinctual part of me wanted me to curl up beside him and bask in his presence, but I couldn't bring myself to voice that desire.

My bear growled, annoyed at me for denying us the closeness we needed.

"Can I come back?" he asked, adjusting his leather jacket as if the action would stop me from detecting the sour scent of his nerves.

Some mate I was.

My alpha was no doubt fighting his urges to claim me in order to respect my wishes, and I hadn't even made him feel like he'd be welcome to return.

"I'd like that," I whispered.

He nodded, and turned to the side. I studied his profile, noting the dark circles under his eyes and the strain bracketing his mouth. He looked rough. Was that because of the scare, or was my continued rejection of our bond weighing on him?

Shifters weren't supposed to delay mating if we were lucky enough to find our fated partner. Most fated pairs would bond within a day or two and work out the details afterward, trusting in the gods to have sent them their perfect other half. This waiting we were doing wasn't natural.

My fear overrode my own mating urges, but Knox didn't have the same trouble. He was keeping his distance by willpower alone.

Guilt churned in my gut. That wasn't fair to him. But I didn't know what else to do. The thought of simply mating with him and trusting in the gods made me feel sick. What if he ended up being just as violent and controlling as Rex?

I closed my eyes so I didn't have to watch him leave. With my enhanced hearing, I could make out every word as Everett escorted him to the door and warned him not to push me when I was already vulnerable. As if he would. Bitterness welled within me. If he'd been going to do that, he'd have done it already.

No, he was being patient. Even when it hurt him.

I gritted my teeth. If I were someone different—someone better—he wouldn't be suffering alone right now, and nor would I.

Light knuckles rapped on the bedroom door. "Danny?"

My eyes flew open. "Milo. When did you get here?"

Milo padded inside on socked feet. "Just now."

Damn. I must have been angsting internally for longer than I'd thought.

"Did you see Knox on the way out?" I asked.

"Yes." He dropped into the chair and rested his forearms on his thighs.

He looked about to ask after me, but I spoke before he could. "What do you think of him? Can I trust him?"

Milo was a good judge of character. He'd had a difficult life and sorting trustworthy people from untrustworthy ones had been a matter of survival for him.

Milo nibbled on his lower lip, his bright eyes angled downward as he thought. "I think..."

"Yeah?" I prompted.

He drew in a deep breath. "I think Knox is someone who knows what he wants and goes for it. In this case, you're the thing he wants."

A thrill shot through me.

I knew that. Of course I did. But somehow, hearing it still delighted my bear.

Mate.

"I don't think he'd hurt you," Milo continued, rubbing his palms on his jeans. "But his sense of morality might not be the same as yours."

He had a good point there. I'd never aid in a kidnapping, but Knox had. He'd helped Tomas kidnap Milo for payment, even if he'd had second thoughts later.

"Do you think I should give him a chance?" I wanted to, but I didn't know if I could bring myself to risk it.

Milo smiled sadly. "I can't make that decision for you."

CHAPTER

# TEN

K NOX
I drew air into my lungs, savoring the honeyed scent of my mate. His breaths were slow and even, and it sounded as if he was sleeping peacefully. I pressed myself against the side of the house, using it as shelter from the wind. It was dark and growing colder with each passing minute.

Inside his bedroom, Danny whimpered. My gut tightened. Was he having a nightmare? My instincts screamed at me to smash the window, leap inside, and comfort him.

*Mate in trouble.*

*Hold mate.*

I resisted the urge. Acting on it would only traumatize Danny more than he already was.

A bird cried from the branches of a tree on the edge of the woods. I didn't recognize the call, but it provided a much-needed distraction. My wolf didn't understand why we were out here instead of inside with our mate. Every time I laid eyes on the gorgeous bear shifter, it became more difficult to fight the beast within me that wanted to claim him.

When Danny smiled at me across the counter in the bakery and handed me the coffee he'd mocked as being "sludge," I ached to kiss him. Each time he said something particularly thoughtful or clever in a text message, my teeth descended, preparing to bite him and make him mine.

The constant struggle was tearing me apart, and I'd hardly been sleeping because of it. I couldn't help but worry that it might tip me over the edge into becoming feral. I'd managed to maintain my sanity when I'd been cast from my pack, but I might not survive being rejected by my mate.

A twig snapped.

I froze, my ears pricked, all senses on high alert.

A scuffle.

Footsteps drew closer.

"It's just me," a deep voice murmured.

A figure rounded the corner of the house.

Everett.

He was carrying something. He set a container on the ground a few yards away. I rose to my feet and sniffed. Spicy meat. Potatoes. Something green.

"I figured I'd find you here." Everett straightened and gestured at the container. "Dinner. From Momma."

I tilted my head. The Clan Alpha's wife had saved a meal for me?

"And a blanket." Everett shook the blanket out and laid it over my back. "I doubt it will do much, but it's better than nothing."

He stood there. Not moving. I allowed a shift to roll through me. As my human form emerged, I wrapped the blanket around myself. Not for the sake of modesty, but for warmth. This form wasn't as well insulated as the other.

"Thank you."

He shrugged. "I know there's no talking you out of guard duty, so it's the least we could do."

I eyeballed him. "It's not as if I could leave my mate unprotected."

"I know." He lowered himself to the ground and sat, cross-legged. "I'd do the same, in your place."

I picked up the container; it was still warm. I cracked open the lid. Focusing on food was easier than making sense of this unexpected gesture of acceptance. Considering how they'd kept their distance, I hadn't thought Danny's family approved of me, but perhaps there was some hope.

After all, Everett had the most reason to dislike me. If he could see past that, surely the others would too, in time.

"I'm sure I'm not what you all want for Danny." There was a knife and fork inside the container, and I used the fork to scoop a fluffy dollop of mashed potatoes into my mouth.

Everett hummed in the back of his throat. "All we want is someone who will love him, protect him, and treat him well. If that's you, then we don't care about anything else."

"If he agrees to be mine, I'll protect him with my life." A shiver rippled down my spine. If Danny was awake, he'd be able to hear every word I said, but I had no problem with that. As long as he didn't think it was creepy that I was staking out his home.

Everett flipped his hood up. "Then we'll figure the rest out."

Thank the gods.

"How's Milo?" I asked, needing to change the subject. I could only handle so much baring of my soul at a time.

Everett chuffed. Or rather, his bear did.

"He's great. A little sick, but improving. I've heard the first trimester is usually the worst for morning sickness."

"Are you going to find out the gender?" I asked.

"No. We decided we'd like it to be a surprise. Besides, the baby might decide they don't want to be defined by their biology, so it makes sense not to hinge so much on whatever they're born with."

"True." I liked that perspective. It was different from what I was used to. My father had been backward in many ways, and certainly wouldn't consider accepting anyone outside of usual gender norms. As it was, he'd struggled with my preference for men over women.

"Do you know if the baby will be a shifter?" I asked.

Everett nodded. "The doctor says they have a shifter's resting heart rate, and the blood test showed proteins that are present in higher quantities in shifters than non-shifters." He glanced at me. "Do you want children?"

My breath hitched. "If I have a stable home and a loving mate. I wouldn't want to raise a baby alone on the road."

"Hmm."

I shoveled more potatoes into my mouth and began slicing the meatballs alongside it, then served myself a piece of one.

Everett watched me steadily. "How long will you wait for Danny?"

I almost choked on the meatball. Eyes watering, I forced myself to chew and swallow. My throat ached as the lump of meat traveled down it. I set the cutlery down and bit back my immediate response of "as long as it takes."

The truth was, I couldn't wait for Danny forever. Not without endangering him. Eventually, my wolf would surface at the wrong time and I risked claiming him without consent. I refused to do that. Even the thought of it filled me with dread.

Furthermore, I wouldn't stay somewhere indefinitely if I wasn't wanted. I'd done that before, and I'd learned my lesson.

"I'm not sure," I admitted, hoping with all my heart that Danny was dead asleep and not listening to us. The soft rise and fall of his breathing was still even. "A few months, maybe."

There was only so long I could expose myself to him without risking the wolf inside overcoming my human respect for Danny's boundaries.

# ELEVEN

**D**ANNY

A rustle outside alerted me to the fact I wasn't alone. I sighed, knowing before I even inhaled his scent that Knox was once again positioned below my bedroom window like some kind of sentinel, just as he had been for the last two nights.

A twinge of guilt pinched my gut. I should let him in. He was out there to protect me, suffering through the discomfort of the hard ground and the cold for my sake. Yet I still hadn't been brave enough to invite him into the house.

I gritted my teeth. Tonight, that changed. I'd made myself a promise earlier that I'd find my courage and do the right thing for once.

Heart pounding, I undid the window latch and pushed it open. Cool air flowed through the gap, solidifying my certainty that I shouldn't leave him outside for yet another night.

"You can come in and use the spare bed," I murmured. I didn't need to speak loudly for him to hear me.

There was a pause, likely while Knox shifted from his furry form to his human one.

"I'm fine out here." His voice rasped, like he was out of practice speaking.

"It must be nicer in here than out there," I pointed out, grateful he remained kneeling and didn't stand. I wasn't sure if I'd be able to face the full glory of his naked body without my bear deciding to take drastic action. "I have a good heating system."

"Shifters run hot," he reminded me.

I growled under my breath. "Just come in. I won't sleep if I know you're out there in the cold."

He made a sound of exasperation. "Fine."

I smirked as he shifted back and trotted around the house. I should have known that would do the trick. Most alphas wanted nothing more than for their omega to be taken care of. He considered me his, so he wouldn't want me to suffer through a sleepless night.

I went to the front door and opened it. Knox walked in. His wolf was massive, with intense green eyes, dark fur that verged on black, and a shoulder that came halfway up my torso. I closed the door, locked it, and turned to face him.

He nudged my hand. I hesitated, then ran my fingers through the shaggy hair on top of his head. Shifters often didn't like to be petted, but mates were a different story, and he seemed to like the affection. He arched into my touch, then pulled away and padded down the hall.

When he returned, on two legs, a towel was wrapped around his waist. There wasn't much point in him covering up, since I'd already seen him naked, but I appreciated his respect for my boundaries and his attempt to keep things between us from turning sexual.

"I'm not sleeping in the spare bedroom," he said, his chin raised. "It's too far away. I'll sleep on the floor outside your room."

I sighed. So much for making him more comfortable. I

supposed at least he'd be out of the elements. "Let me get you a mattress."

I dragged the mattress off the spare bed and into the hall. Knox hovered, apparently unsure what to do.

"The floor would have been fine," he said, running his hand through his hair. "I've slept in worse places."

My chest ached. Perhaps he had, but I didn't like to think of it. I may not be ready to accept him as my mate, but nor did I want to think of his life being anything other than wonderful. Although obviously, bad things must have happened to him. Why else would he bother to stick around, waiting for a useless mate like me?

Low self-esteem was the only answer I could think of.

"Not on my watch," I muttered, pushing the mattress against the wall. "Will this do?"

He nodded, and fingered the edge of the towel, capturing my gaze. His torso was firm, banded with muscle. I followed the ridges of his abdomen up to his chest. Scar tissue was knotted over his heart.

My insides chilled. It was almost impossible to scar a shifter, and I wanted to ask what had caused it, but I hadn't earned the right to pry.

"Lock the door." Knox lowered himself onto the mattress and crossed his legs. My eyes snapped up to his face. "I want you to feel safe."

My heart skipped. I hated that he knew his presence both reassured me and unnerved me, but I was grateful he was encouraging me to do what I needed.

"I'll be right through the wall." I hesitated. "Do you need anything?"

His dark eyes watched me intently. "No. I have everything I need."

A shiver rippled through me. I got the impression he wasn't referring to the mattress or shelter. He meant me.

"Good night." I darted inside the bedroom and closed the door, then flicked the lock into place.

"Sleep well, Danny," Knox murmured.

My insides warmed. As I climbed into bed, my bear whined internally, demanding to know why we were leaving our mate on the wrong side of the door.

We're not ready yet, I told him.

He didn't understand. He wanted Knox now.

I snuggled beneath the covers, closed my eyes, and listened to Knox's heartbeat. His presence, albeit at a distance, soothed my bear. I tuned out everything except for the steady thump and allowed it to lull me to sleep.

When I woke, gray light filtered into the room around the edges of the curtains. I glanced at my phone. It was a little past 8 a.m., and I wasn't due at the bakery for another few hours yet. Closing my eyes again, I focused on the noises outside the bedroom and immediately realized that Knox was no longer in the house.

My heart sank. Even if I hadn't admitted it to myself, I'd been looking forward to seeing him. I threw back the covers, climbed out of bed, and pulled on a pair of sweatpants and a T-shirt before unlocking and opening the bedroom door. The mattress was no longer on the floor against the wall. He must have returned it to the spare room.

I walked on bare feet down the hall and into the living area. The delicious scent of coffee greeted me. A pot had been recently brewed, and a full mug was waiting beside it. I leaned over the mug and sniffed, catching the scent of something sweeter. Caramel. A grin swept across my face. He'd remembered.

I lifted the mug of coffee. Beneath it was a note.

*Look in the fridge.*

Intrigued, I carried the coffee to the fridge and looked

inside. A small platter was arranged inside with a pastry, sliced fruit, and a small bowl of berries and yogurt.

Tears sprang to my eyes. How sweet. I couldn't believe he'd done this. Especially after I'd made him sleep in the hall and had apparently been so unwelcoming he didn't think he could stay and join me for breakfast—a meal that he'd prepared.

Why was I like this?

I gritted my teeth. I knew why. I just didn't know how to fix it.

Taking the coffee and tray to the dining table, I sat and ate. The coffee was just the right amount of sweet, and I felt slightly better once my belly was full.

I showered, dressed in jeans and a green short-sleeved shirt that flattered my complexion, then locked up and headed down the street to Everett and Milo's house. I knocked and waited for Milo to answer. Everett would already be at work by now.

As soon as Milo opened the door, I fell into his arms. They closed around me and he patted my back.

He made the kind of shushing noises people used to soothe distraught babies. "What's wrong?"

"I'm a terrible mate."

He drew back, frowning. "No, you're not."

"But I—"

He stopped me with a finger to my lips. "Come in and sit down, then you can tell me."

He closed the door and ushered me to their sofa. I sat and he dropped onto the cushion beside me, keeping close in case I needed him. My heart lifted. I was so lucky that Everett had found such a wonderful partner.

I released a stuttered breath and it all burst from me. How Knox had been guarding my window. The fact I'd invited him in but made him sleep on the hall floor. The way he'd prepared me breakfast so thoughtfully and left. My worries that I'd made him feel unwanted.

Milo took my hand in his. "Are you interested in Knox? If not for Rex, would you want to get to know him better?"

I thought for a moment, then nodded. "I would. He's patient and protective. He's been nothing but considerate of me. I just need…"

"Time," he finished for me. "Which means you need him to stay around here for long enough to build trust."

"Yeah." I was scared he'd give up on me and leave when I knew we could have something good if only I'd get over my hang-ups.

Milo nibbled on his lower lip. "Can I make a suggestion?"

"Of course." It surprised me that he had to ask.

"Perhaps a good first step would be to encourage the clan to be more accepting of him. Some members have been keeping him at a distance or excluding him because they think that's what you want."

A sour taste formed on the back of my tongue. "They have?" Oh, gods. He was lingering in Grizzly Ridge solely because of me, and yet I was responsible for people treating him poorly. My gut roiled, and I felt sick. "Tell me who."

CHAPTER

# TWELVE

**K***NOX*
I was walking down the main street, on my way to the bakery for my now-routine daily coffee, when I noticed the throng of people outside one of the shops. They jittered with nervous energy and were muttering amongst themselves, keeping their voices so low that only those with enhanced hearing could decipher them.

I frowned as my nose filled with the bitter scent of fear. I headed for the nearest people—an older couple. The woman was carrying a paper bag from the bakery.

"What's going on?" I asked.

They turned to me. Her eyes widened with surprise, but his didn't so I assumed he'd heard me coming.

"There's been a break-in at the hardware store." He crossed his arms, scowling fiercely. "They've been robbed."

I stiffened. Perhaps elsewhere a break-in wouldn't be out of the ordinary, but I'd been under the impression that Grizzly Ridge had a very low crime rate.

The woman wrung her hands. "Between this and the incident at the bakery, people are scared."

"You think they're related?"

She stepped closer to her partner. "Things like this don't happen around here."

No. I hadn't thought so.

"Thanks for filling me in." I nodded to them and continued along the street, drawing nearer to the hardware shop.

One of the deputies—Clay, if I recalled right—was standing guard outside the store to stop rubberneckers from getting inside.

He shifted position as I approached. "Sorry, man, but I can't let you in."

I stopped in front of him. "Smells like wolf."

He hesitated, then nodded.

"You know I spent some time in Moonlight Cove. If it was the wolves there that did this, then I'll recognize their scents."

He glanced over his shoulder, visibly uncertain. "I don't know..."

"Ask Zander."

Clay reached for his phone and dialed a number. "Boss? It's Clay. We've got that wolf shifter mercenary out here. Says he might be able to recognize the scents." He waited while Zander replied, then hung up and jerked his thumb toward the door. "You can go in. Just don't touch anything."

"Thanks." I stepped inside through the door and into a dimly lit space with a concrete floor and rows of shelves extending almost all the way across from one wall to the other, with a narrow space to walk on the far side and a wider space on this side.

"Knox." Zander stepped in front of me and tipped his hat. "What do you smell?"

I closed my eyes and breathed in, filtering through the

layers of scent, mentally categorizing most as belonging to the Grizzly Ridge clan. A few stood out as being different.

"It was definitely wolves from Moonlight Cove," I told him. "Two of them were in human form; the other was shifted, and judging from his scent, I'd say he's on the verge of turning feral. Do you smell that hint of rotten meat?"

Zander breathed in deeply. "I do. Damn. I hope like hell they returned to Moonlight Cove and aren't lying low around here somewhere. A wolf in that state could be dangerous."

"His pack must be able to control him if they brought him with them." It may not be much, but it was something at least. There was little worse than an out-of-control feral shifter. "Do you think this is related to the bakery incident and that break-in at the cabin?"

Zander's lips pressed together. "I'm afraid I can't share the details of a police investigation with a civilian."

My gut clenched. "Come on," I growled. "I'm trying to help you."

"And you have." He removed his hat and held it over his chest. "The best thing you can do now is go and get your coffee and carry on with your day. If and when I can share, I will, but not now."

My jaw tightened, and my back teeth ground together. My fists clenched and my claws threatened to emerge, but by power of will, I held back the partial shift. Tilting my chin in acknowledgment, I strode away before I could say anything I'd regret later.

The crowd was still gathered outside, and many of them watched me with a combination of interest and caution as I left the shop and struggled to get my emotions under control. No doubt they could smell the strength of my turmoil and wanted to know what had caused it.

I drew in a deep breath and released it slowly. Perhaps I

could use their interest to my benefit. Zander may have stonewalled me from the police investigation, but I wasn't ready to drop this. The rogue wolf pack was showing far too much interest in Grizzly Ridge.

My mate lived here. I had to make sure he was safe. The last thing Danny needed was another reason to be scared.

With that in mind, I made my way to a cluster of three middle-aged shifters chatting quietly on the opposite side of the street.

"Have you gentlemen heard anything about what happened?" I asked, doing my best to come across as charming and unthreatening and probably failing.

The one on the left's eyes narrowed. "You're that wolf shifter. Aren't you part of the rogue pack?"

His words hit like a punch. I tilted my face toward the sky so he wouldn't see that they hurt. When I'd gathered myself, I looked at him again.

"No." I spoke firmly and clearly. "I'm not. What do you know?"

The man didn't respond, but one of his companions fidgeted so I turned toward him.

"The cops arrived about forty minutes ago," he said, shooting a sidelong glance at his friends. "I was on my way to work and I didn't hear anything before then, so maybe the hardware store has a silent alarm."

"Thanks." Considering his buddy's suspicion, this was more information than I'd expected to get. "I'm Knox, by the way."

"Ray."

We shook hands.

"I'm due to get coffee." I wouldn't inflict my presence on them for longer than necessary.

I trudged toward the bakery, my heart heavy as I wondered whether I'd ever be completely welcome here, or if my name would always be tainted by association with Tomas and the rogue wolf pack.

A few minutes later, I arrived outside the bakery and looked in through the window. Danny was behind the counter, jotting something on a piece of paper. He looked up and we locked eyes. Slowly, he raised his hand and waved.

My heart lurched. Such a simple gesture, and yet it filled me with hope for a future with him that I'd hardly dared to envision.

Gods. Either I was a lucky son of a bitch, or I was setting myself up for a fall that I might never recover from.

*Don't break me, Danny.*

# THIRTEEN

*D*ANNY

"Do you think Knox will come?" I asked Milo as we carried platters of food through my parents' house and out the back doors onto the deck.

There was a pack run tonight, and I'd been both dreading it and looking forward to it all week. I was eager to see Knox in his other form and to spend more time with him, but I was also anxious about achieving my mission.

I needed to make it clear to the clan that I cared for Knox so they shouldn't ostracize him on my behalf. That wasn't fair. Especially not when he was the one already being hurt by a reluctant mate.

"Do you want him to come?" Milo asked, setting down a platter on one of the tables arranged along the side of the deck. The outdoor lights were on, although most shifters wouldn't need the artificial illumination to see the food properly.

"Yeah." The admission was easier than I'd expected. "I do."

Milo straightened and turned away from the table, his

gaze catching on something behind me. He flashed me a smile. "Behind you."

I looked around and my breath caught. Knox was standing in the doorway, his silhouette framed by the light spilling from inside. Shadows danced across his stubbled jaw and hid his eyes from view. Although I couldn't see them, I got the feeling he was looking straight at me.

I shivered. Fuck, he was sexy.

"Go," Milo hissed, giving my shoulder a little push. "You've got this."

Did I?

I didn't feel like it.

But I couldn't just stare at Knox all night, so I gathered my courage and forced myself into motion. A moment later, I found myself in front of him.

"Danny." His tone was warm and slightly raspy. Incredibly masculine.

"Knox." I loved the way his name tasted on my tongue. "What's your favorite bakery item?"

His eyebrows knitted together. "Why do you want to know?"

I kept my chin high. "Because I'd like to properly thank you for protecting me after those wolves drove through the bakery window, and for keeping an eye on me every night since then."

The slightest hint of a blush appeared on his cheeks. "You don't have to give me anything. I was happy to do it."

"I insist." I wasn't about to back down now that I was finally being brave enough to have a proper conversation with him that didn't involve either an exchange of cash for coffee or some kind of trauma.

He chuckled. "Suit yourself. I like apple pie."

"Excellent." I'd make him the best apple pie he'd ever eaten.

"Excuse me, boys."

I started. I hadn't noticed Momma hovering behind Knox, trying to get through the doorway. "Sorry, Momma."

Knox stepped aside, and I moved with him. Momma joined us on the deck, and Dad whistled to get everyone's attention. Once he had it, he injected a little Alpha boom into his voice and spoke loudly enough for us all to hear.

"Thank you for coming to our first run of December. I won't talk for long because I can see you've all been helping yourself to Melinda's excellent cooking and are eager to burn off some energy in the woods. Next time we meet, we'll be well into the festive season. I know you're looking forward to it. I certainly am. Stay safe tonight. Keep away from humans. And most of all, have fun."

He fell silent, and after a couple of seconds, the hum of conversation restarted. Behind me, I could hear George and Sam from the children's home chatting about the events they had planned, and to my left, the owner of the general store was making plans to put up decorations with his wife.

I sauntered over to them and joined in the conversation. When the opportunity presented itself, I asked if they'd met Knox. They were both wary, and I felt a twinge of guilt. If I'd been more aware of the situation, I could have ensured that Knox was made to feel welcome from the beginning, despite my uncertainty as to what to do about him.

I hurried to explain how protective he was of me, and how we were getting to know each other. When they seemed to have gotten the point, I moved on to another group. I cycled in and out of different conversations, mentioning Knox and praising him in ways that I knew shifters would approve of.

One of the older bear shifters asked why I'd rejected him if he was so great.

I flinched, and curled in on myself. "I'm afraid that has

more to do with my own poor past decisions than it does with him," I admitted, feeling two feet tall.

Understanding dawned in his expression.

"That no-good Rex," he growled, opening his mouth as if about to begin a tirade. However, at that point, Knox materialized at my side.

"Are you okay?" he asked. "You look upset."

I blinked, surprised that he'd picked up on my mood from across the deck. "I'm fine."

Knox frowned. "Are you sure?"

"Perfectly."

"He is," my companion confirmed. "He was just singing your praises."

Patches of red appeared on Knox's cheeks. "Uh, the others are getting ready to run. Would you like to too?"

I looked around and realized that he was right. While I'd been busy glad-handing on his behalf, others had begun to strip off their clothes and head into the woods.

"Yeah, sounds good."

The bear shifter we were with stretched onto his tiptoes and scanned the crowd. "Damn, my wife has already left. I'm gonna be in trouble later."

He rushed away. Knox led me to the end of the deck. He kicked off his shoes, removed his socks, and was undoing the fly of his jeans by the time I realized that I was staring without actually doing anything myself.

He glanced at me and raised an eyebrow. One side of his mouth hitched in a smirk, as if silently asking whether I wanted him to reveal more. I wasn't ready for that yet so I tore my gaze away and focused on undressing myself. Shoes came off, followed by socks, jeans, and my sweater.

I peeked at Knox. His legs were bare now, and damn they were sexy. Muscular thighs, juicy calves, and nestled at the top, a cock that was long and thick and made my mouth water.

Focus, Danny.

I pulled off my shirt and, feeling suddenly shy, turned away as I yanked down my underwear. I shifted quickly, eager to get into my fur. When I looked back around, Knox was gone and in his place stood an enormous wolf with glossy black fur and gleaming green eyes.

My breath caught. He was beautiful.

He met my gaze and I couldn't help but wonder what he saw when he looked at me. My fur was thick and richly colored, and I took good care of myself, but Knox was a wolf. He wouldn't necessarily find the same things attractive that other bears did. What did he think of me?

He nudged me with his muzzle, and jerked his head toward the woods. He wanted to join the others. I lumbered toward the trees but stopped when he ran in front of me and danced in a circle. His head was low to the ground, his backside up in the air, his tail wagging.

All of a sudden, he took off. He wanted to play.

I gave chase. I followed him into the woods, winding between trees, allowing the swish of his dark tail to lead me farther into the depths of the national park.

When he left my side, I used scent to guide me until I realized that he had doubled around. I turned and found him behind me. He yipped and bounced. I chuffed at him and nosed his side. He pounced, and I rolled onto my back. I should have been scared, having my belly exposed to a predator, but I felt safe.

Maybe we could make this work after all.

Just as I was considering shifting so I could talk to him properly, the bush rustled behind us and Everett burst into the clearing.

I sighed. Any conversation would have to wait.

CHAPTER

# FOURTEEN

K*NOX*

As soon as I'd donned my clothes, I searched for Danny. We had been having such fun earlier, before Everett had arrived, or at least I thought we had been. Now, in hindsight, I wondered if I hadn't overstepped by trying to play with him. He'd been keeping me at a distance, and my wolf had ignored that, wanting to engage in typical mating fun.

"Hey," I said, approaching Danny from behind, and doing my best to ignore the expanse of silky pale skin as he slid his shirt over his head and turned with his sweater in hand. "Can we talk for a moment?"

"Sure." He cocked his head. "What's the matter?"

"I'm sorry if I pushed you earlier." I tugged on the end of my ponytail. "I shouldn't have come on so strong."

Danny pursed his lips. "You didn't push me, and I hate that you have to be so cautious with me. I enjoyed our time together in our other forms. It was nice to play, and for it just to be simple." He heaved a sigh. "I'm sorry that I'm not easy. Almost any other mate would be less work than I am. I am... complicated. I wish I wasn't because you deserve better."

I shook my head. "You're perfect as you are. I never want you to feel rushed, or like you have to follow someone else's timeframe."

He buried his face in his hands and growled. "I just hate how hard this must be for you. I'm sorry. I'm so, so sorry."

"Hey, now." Gently, I laid my hand on his shoulder. "Take it easy on yourself. I never want you to be sorry for being the way you are. I'm not sorry to have met my mate, and you shouldn't be either just because our path forward isn't as clear as it might otherwise be. You're giving me a chance, and that means more to me than you could possibly imagine."

Danny's expression softened. "Thank you."

He glanced down, and his eyes widened. I pretended not to notice that he was eyeballing my crotch. Yes, I was aroused. Unfortunately, when I was around him, that tended to be the case. It didn't mean I was going to act on it.

"Can I walk you home?" I asked.

Danny blushed. "I'd like that."

He pulled his sweater on and sat to put on his shoes and tie his laces. When he stood, he offered me his arm. I linked mine with it, and drew him close, subtly breathing in his sweet, honeyed scent.

We bid goodbye to our hosts and circled around the house and onto the street. I walked him a couple of doors down to his own place, and accompanied him all the way to the door.

On the doorstep, I untangled my arm from his and stepped back.

"You aren't coming in?" he asked.

I understood the question. I'd been standing watch over

him most nights. But nothing had happened for a while, and unfortunately, although I could ignore my arousal while in Danny's presence, it needed to be dealt with. I could hardly jerk off in his hallway. Even if he didn't hear me, he'd smell it.

"Not this time, I'm afraid."

"Oh." Danny looked down at his hands. "It's not because..."

"It has nothing to do with you," I assured him. "There's something I need to take care of at home."

Relief lightened his features. "Okay, then."

We looked into each other's eyes for a long moment. Just as I was about to turn away, he grabbed the lapel of my jacket and pulled me close.

Then, he kissed me.

His lips were soft against mine, and he smelled of sugar and earth. I groaned and shifted against him, edging closer. Cautiously, I darted my tongue out to taste his lips. A hint of something spicy lingered from his earlier meal but the rest was pure Danny.

He sagged against me. I circled my arms around him, but instantly, he stiffened. Immediately, I let him go. I backed up with my hands held in front of me, placating.

"It's okay," I said. "You're safe."

I don't know how I knew that's what he needed to hear, but I did.

He hauled in a shuddering breath. "Sorry."

"What did we say about being sorry?" I demanded.

He shuffled from one foot to the other. "That I shouldn't be?"

"Damn right." He had nothing to be sorry for. I shouldn't have grabbed him. I should have taken what he was giving me and let him lead.

He narrowed his eyes. "Well, neither should you. I liked

that." He flushed. "A lot. So don't feel guilty. I'll see you tomorrow?"

"You will." Even if it was just for my daily coffee order.

I said good night and hurried away before I changed my mind and ended up dozing beneath his windowsill again. I traveled back to my place on foot. I hadn't ridden my motorcycle to the gathering because I still worried that it might scare Danny. One day, I'd take him riding on the back, but for now, baby steps were needed.

When I arrived at the cabin, I let myself in, locked the door, and started the shower. I stripped off and stuck my hand in to test the temperature of the water. When it was warm enough, I got in.

Closing my eyes, I savored the beat of the water against my back and wrapped my hand around my cock. Traces of Danny's scent lingered on my skin, and I summoned an image of him to the forefront of my mind just as he'd been earlier. Naked in the moonlight, his lean muscles dancing as he moved.

Fuck, he was sexy.

I pumped my hand along my cock, twisting at the end, rubbing my thumb on the underside of the sensitive head. My hand was too big. Too rough. Danny's would be smaller, with fine fingers and soft skin. Never mind. This would have to do for now.

Shuttling my hand back and forth, I imagined him in the throes of passion. His lips would part on a cry, the cords of his neck would stand out, and that cock—the one I so badly wanted to touch—would drip with evidence of how badly he wanted me.

My dick throbbed and I threw my head back, roaring as I came. Cum splattered the shower wall. I panted, catching my breath.

Gods, if this was what happened when I jerked off to a

fantasy of Danny, then I wasn't sure I was prepared for how strongly my body might react when I actually had him in my arms. When that time came, he'd better be damn sure about us, because once I had him, I doubted I'd be able to let him go.

I rinsed off the wall, washed myself, and shut the shower off. I dried myself with brisk movements and checked my phone. A message from Danny awaited.

**Danny:** *Come by the bakery on Monday morning.*

# FIFTEEN

*D*ANNY
My gut swam with nerves as I opened the oven and pulled out the pie tin I'd used to make apple pie this morning. I hoped Knox would like it. My family loved apple pie and this was my special recipe.

A snick sounded in the silence of the bakery and I jumped in surprise. I spun around, searching for the source of the noise but saw nothing.

Damn, I hated being here by myself in the morning and the evening. After the run-in with Rex and the incident with the car driving through the front window, I felt I had the right to be nervous.

Metal scraped on metal. I placed the apple pie on a board on the countertop and silently closed the oven. Then I tiptoed through the kitchen and peered into the main section of the bakery. A figure was framed by the dim street lights, standing only about five and a half feet tall against the glass of the door.

I relaxed. It was Skye. Thank the gods.

She opened the door and shuffled inside, her handbag

slung over one shoulder. Her familiar scent—cinnamon and freshly baked bread—comforted me.

"You gave me a fright," I said, working to calm my breathing.

She glanced over. "Sorry, I wasn't trying to be sneaky."

"I know." I rubbed my chest, easing the tension there. "I wasn't paying attention, that's all."

She grinned. "Too busy daydreaming about your hot mate?"

I snorted. She was closer to the truth than she knew. I'd been waiting since Saturday for the chance to impress Knox with a treat made especially for him. Now that the day had arrived, I just hoped he'd get here soon so that I wouldn't have to be anxious for long.

"Oh." Her grin widened. "I'm right, aren't I?"

"Maybe a little. But this is the only time I'll ever admit it."

She sniffed. "Is that apple pie I smell? I didn't think we were making any today."

I headed for the kitchen and heard her trail behind me. "It's for Knox."

"Aww." The joy in her voice warmed me. She was genuinely happy for me. "So, any news there?"

I set a timer to allow the pie to cool before I took it out of the case. "Nothing major. I just wanted to do something nice for him."

"I get that." Her tone had changed, growing serious. "If I found my mate, I'd want to do nice things for them too."

I turned to her. "You will soon."

"Gods, I hope so." Her tone was wistful. If anyone deserved a mate, it was Skye. She was so sweet, and so caring to everyone she met.

"You'll meet your alpha soon," I promised. "They're out there and I'm sure they're trying to find you."

She dismissed my comment with a wave of her hand. "Enough sentimental stuff. Let's get to work."

For the next hour or so, we went through our usual daily tasks, getting everything set up for a busy morning. Mondays were often chaotic as everyone got back into work for the week.

When the doorbell sounded a little after nine in the morning, I didn't think anything of it until the enticing notes of pine and leather reached my nose. Then my pulse skittered. Knox was here.

I rushed out of the kitchen, bustling past Skye, who was making coffee, and hurried around the kitchen counter. "Hi!"

"Danny." A smile stretched Knox's full lower lip. "Good morning."

"You came." I felt silly as soon as the words were out of my mouth. He'd said he would, so of course he had. I shouldn't be surprised. And yet, I'd grown used to Rex failing to keep commitments he'd made to me.

Honestly, it was shocking that he'd had the audacity to accuse me of being unfaithful, considering that I'd had far more reason to be suspicious of his fidelity than vice versa.

"I did." He glanced at Skye. "I don't want to keep you from your work though."

"It's his break time," she said, presenting the man at the counter with a coffee. There was only one other person waiting. Most of the early morning rush had already been through. "You've got fifteen minutes."

I blew her a kiss. "Thanks, Skye. Can I get you a drink, Knox?"

He nodded. "You know what I like."

I did, and a primal sense of satisfaction welled up inside me because of it.

I knew how to satisfy my alpha's coffee craving.

I prepared his usual double-shot espresso and made myself a caramel latte with whipped cream, then carried them both to a table in the corner of the bakery.

"I'll be back in a moment," I told him. "Sit."

I darted back into the kitchen, readied my surprise, and carried it out to him, brimming with excitement and nerves.

His eyes widened as I approached. "Is that..."

"Apple pie," I declared, setting it in front of him with a flourish. "With whipped cream and apple spice."

"Mm." He breathed it in and his eyes flashed green. "Smells delicious."

Somehow, I didn't think he was only talking about the pie. My cock plumped a little. I sat opposite him before it became obvious, although he could probably smell my arousal anyway.

He scooped up a portion of the pie with a spoon, gathered cream on the end, and popped it into his mouth, holding my gaze as he chewed. Green flickered in his eyes again, and his nostrils flared.

Yeah, he definitely knew what he was doing to me.

He withdrew the spoon from his mouth. "This is the best apple pie I've ever had." His rough voice heated my blood. He scooped up more of the dessert and offered it to me. "Have some."

I stared at the spoon. Was I seriously going to let him hand-feed me?

Without conscious thought, my lips closed around the spoon and the sweet/tart combination of apples and sugar melted on my tongue.

Apparently, I was.

His eyes flared brighter, and this time, the intense green color lingered. I drew back and drank my coffee, grateful to have a break from his intensity. This definitely wasn't the right place for my libido to reawaken.

I cleared my throat. "Have you had any luck finding a job?"

His irises turned brown again. "Not yet."

"Sorry to hear it." I'd have to work harder to get the locals to embrace him.

He shrugged. "It's fine. I have enough free time to look into a few troubling goings-on in the area."

My eyebrows drew together. What did he mean? I wanted to ask, but something gave me the impression he wouldn't answer.

"Be careful," I warned him. I was only just getting to know him, but I still didn't want anything happening to him. My bear shifted restlessly inside at the thought.

*Protect mate.*

I almost laughed at the notion. I couldn't even protect myself. How the hell was I supposed to protect an alpha wolf?

"I will."

We chatted for a while longer, but when Skye reminded me that my break was over, I had to return behind the counter. Knox left, but he paused outside and looked back in through the recently repaired window to smile at me.

My heart hammered, and I silently promised myself to make sure he had all the apple pie he ever wanted. Feeding him was one of the only ways I could care for him at the moment, so I'd make the most of it.

I got busy serving customers, and it wasn't until the pre-lunch lull that I realized Knox hadn't mentioned seeing me again soon.

"What if he's getting tired of me holding back?" I asked Skye.

She propped her chin on her palm and a lock of her hair

fell across her forehead. "Perhaps he's just letting you set the pace. You know, like, waiting for you to go to him."

"Maybe." But I wasn't sure if I was brave enough to do that.

Gods, I was messed up. I didn't want him to push me, but I was too damn cowardly to take the lead myself. What on earth was I supposed to do?

# SIXTEEN

K*NOX*

The persistent vibrating of my phone woke me on Saturday morning. I rolled over and reached blindly for the phone, swiping it off the nightstand. I rolled onto my back and blinked to clear my vision.

"Hello?" My breath fogged in the air, but the room was light so it must be morning.

"Knox?"

I didn't recognize the voice.

"This is Craig from the butcher," he continued, filling the gap. "I've had a break-in overnight. The police are on their way, but Ray told me you were doing your own investigation, and he gave me your number so I could call you too."

I rubbed my palm over my forehead, sweeping my hair off my face. "I'm glad you did. I'll be there soon."

"See you then. I've got to go." Craig hung up.

Summoning a burst of energy, I swung my legs off the edge of the bed and stood. I was pleased Craig had called. I'd been circulating around town, speaking with the locals and digging up as much as I could this past week, but without their cooperation, I doubted I'd get anywhere.

I didn't bother to shower. Any time I delayed would just make it more difficult to get access to the crime scene. Instead, I tugged on the T-shirt, jacket, and jeans I'd worn yesterday, shoved my feet into my heavy boots and rode my Harley into the town center.

Once again, locals were gathered on the street outside the location of the break-in. I parked at the end of the block and cut a path through them until I reached the front door. A different officer stood guard this time. He was shorter and slimmer than Clay, with a slightly hooked nose and eyes a shade of gold that I'd never seen before.

I glanced at his badge. "Good morning, Deputy Hawk."

He cocked his head. There was something very avian about the movement. "It's just Hawk. I'm guessing you want to come in and use that sensitive nose I've heard about."

"That's right." I wasn't surprised that word had gotten around about my nose. Small towns gossiped. It was just a fact of life.

"Just so you know, the sheriff has a good nose too. Now that he's smelled the wolves at the hardware store, he'll recognize their scents if he comes across them again."

I inclined my head in acknowledgment. "I'd still like to check."

"Let him in," Zander called from somewhere behind Hawk. "He's too stubborn to leave. Knox, keep your hands to yourself."

"Will do, Sheriff." I shoved them into my pockets to emphasize the point. I had no interest in jeopardizing their investigation. I just wanted information to fuel my own.

I clomped inside, my boots slapping on the vinyl floor. I made my way around the glass cabinet that would usually display an array of high-end meat products and to the door that led through to the rear of the shop.

The metallic scent of blood and meat disguised the more subtle scents beneath. I sniffed, definitely catching a hint of that rottenness associated with wolves turning feral.

As I entered the workroom at the rear of the building, I came up short. Zander and a female officer were inside, along with a portly red-faced man that I assumed was Craig, the butcher.

What I didn't see was meat.

"How much was taken?" I asked, not bothering with any niceties.

"Everything I had in stock." Craig's voice was thick with frustration, his anger just barely reined in. "I had the shop warded by a warlock after the break-in at the hardware store, but they must have brought a stronger warlock who was able to overcome the wards."

Interesting. I sniffed again. Now that I was paying better attention, I could detect the aroma of ozone that often accompanied magic, accompanied by that of concrete during summer rain, which must be the warlock's personal scent.

"They did," I confirmed, then hesitated over whether to share my suspicions. The break-in at the hardware store could have been random, but this wasn't.

Zander sighed. "What is it?"

"They might be stocking up." I met his gaze. "If they're planning to move on, they'll need supplies, and they could have exhausted whatever was available in Moonlight Cove. They've been bleeding the town dry for months."

Zander scratched his jaw. "You might be right."

"Isn't that good?" the female officer asked. "We want them gone."

"It depends where they're planning to move on to,"

Zander replied before I could. "And what they intend to take with them when they go."

Gods forbid they decided that Grizzly Ridge would be their new home. Hopefully they were smart enough not to come here. A town consisting of primarily bear shifters wouldn't be easy to subdue.

"What do you mean, 'what they intend to take'?" I asked, my brow furrowing. "You think they'll steal more supplies?"

Zander's jaw tightened, and a muscle flexed in it almost imperceptibly. He looked around, then moved closer. When he spoke, it was barely above a whisper.

"We've had reports of strangers lingering outside the Children's Home and the Omega House. This particular wolf pack has been known to kidnap local omegas and..." He trailed off, but I understood where he'd been going, and my blood ran cold.

"I'll stay on guard." No way in hell was I letting them anywhere near Danny.

"Good." He jerked his chin toward the door. "If there's nothing else, you'd better leave. You really shouldn't be here."

"Thanks." I headed out. It would be best not to push him if I wanted him to continue allowing me access to crime scenes.

I circled around the block to avoid any questions from the locals gathered in the street and pulled up Google Maps on my phone. I did a quick search for the location of the Children's Home. It was within walking distance, so I started there on foot.

The Children's Home was located within a large white house with a small plaque out front. The place had a neatly kept front garden—mostly bare, at the moment—and a covered porch. I strode up the paved path and knocked on the front door. It opened quickly, as if someone had been watching me approach.

A skinny kid in the doorway frowned up at me. They were in their mid- to late-teens with bright blue eyes ringed with eyeliner and pale ginger hair. A dark long-sleeved shirt hugged their torso, and a patterned burgundy skirt fell from their hips to the floor.

"Can I help you?" Their voice was soft but wary.

I breathed in subtly. Omega. Fox shifter. "I'm Knox. I'd like to speak to whoever is in charge."

Their bony hip jutted out. "Why?"

"Adult stuff, kid."

"Sam." Their lip curled. "I'm nearly eighteen."

I bit back my impatience. Despite their attitude, Sam's arms were wrapped defensively around their waist and I got the feeling that they were a little scared of me.

"I'm trying to keep the town safe. Is that enough?"

Sam pursed their lips. "Is this about the rogue wolves?"

I struggled to hide my surprise. "What do you know about them?"

Sam shifted from one foot to the other, their skirt swishing. "I've seen a guy hanging around out here, mostly at night. He's tall. Like, maybe six foot two or three. I'm pretty sure he's a wolf because of the way his eyes change when he's trying to see inside."

My insides chilled. "That's exactly the sort of thing I need to hear about." Fear for this vulnerable omega rippled through me. They may be technically still a child, but many shifters would consider seventeen to be old enough to be fair game. "Whatever you do, don't approach him. You hear me?"

Sam nodded. "I wouldn't anyway." They shuddered delicately. "I sense bad juju from him."

"Good." I cleared my throat. "So, the manager?"

Sam pulled a face. "George isn't here. He had to run to the grocery store."

"Oh." And in the meantime, Sam had used the opportunity to try to pump me for information. I had to admire the kid. "I'll be back later then. Tell him to be vigilant, okay?"

"Okay." As I stepped backward, they closed the door.

Returning to the road, I resorted to Google once again to direct me to the Omega House. This was a bit farther away, so I walked back to my motorcycle and rode it toward the south end of town.

There were no vehicles parked outside the large turn-of-the-century style villa. I left my motorcycle by the sidewalk and jogged up the path, rubbing my hands together to warm them. I hadn't thought to grab a pair of gloves before leaving this morning.

I knocked and waited. This time, it took longer for anyone to respond. When the door opened, I hardly managed to conceal my shock. The omega on the other side was the largest I'd ever seen. Over six feet tall, with broad shoulders and muscular biceps.

"Whoever you're looking for, they aren't here," he barked, scowling furiously.

"Um. The manager."

The omega crossed his arms. "You've found him."

I had, and he wasn't anything like what I'd expected. It served me right for making assumptions.

"I just wanted to check whether you've noticed anyone suspicious nearby lately," I said, keeping my tone friendly. "There have been some break-ins, and I'm working with the police to ensure the community's safety."

That was stretching the truth a bit, but it was unavoidable.

The man nodded. "I'll keep the police updated if we notice anything concerning. I'm afraid I can't let you in because you'll frighten the other omegas, and without any formal identification in the form of a badge or a phone call from Sheriff Blackwood, I have nothing else to say to you."

I tempered my annoyance. He was protecting his charges, and I respected that. "Thank you. I'll be around."

As I started to turn away, he called out, "Wait, there is one other thing."

"What's that?" I tried not to sound too interested.

His mouth twitched, leading me to believe I'd failed to appear uninterested. "Good luck with Danny. He deserves to have something good in his life. But you'd better not hurt him, or you and I will have a problem."

"I won't."

He stared me down, and oddly enough, nerves fizzled in my gut. I got the impression that this omega would make a formidable enemy if he decided he didn't like me.

# SEVENTEEN

*DANNY*

I was sitting opposite Everett and Milo at their dinner table, eating a meal that Milo had prepared, when his phone rang. Everett raised an eyebrow, but gestured for Milo to answer.

Flushing, Milo fished it from his pocket and raised the phone to his ear. "Hello?" After a moment, his smile vanished. Slowly, his expression crumpled. "Are you sure? Okay. No. We'll be there soon. Lock all of the doors and stay inside."

He lowered the phone to the table, his cheeks pale.

"What's going on?" Everett asked.

"That was Sam." His voice shook. "George was fixing the Christmas lights strung across the porch—some of the bulbs had gone out—and a car pulled up outside the house. Two alphas got out, pulled him down from the ladder, shoved him in the back of the car and drove away."

"Oh, my gods." I dropped my cutlery with a clatter. "Was he hurt?"

"Sam didn't think so. Apparently, they recognized one of the alphas, although they don't know his name." He rubbed his jaw, obviously distraught. "I can't believe this is happening. Poor George."

I clambered off my chair and hurried around to embrace him. Of course this would hit Milo hard. Only a short time ago, he'd been kidnapped himself. He knew exactly how terrifying it was.

"It'll be okay," I assured him. "Our family will get him back."

Everett was already making a phone call. I kept my arms around Milo as I listened to him speak first to Zander, alerting him to the situation, then to Garrick, and finally, to Dad. Usually, keeping the Alpha informed would take precedence, but since Zander and Garrick were better positioned to start a search, it made sense to notify them first.

"We're going to meet at the Search and Rescue headquarters," Everett said, rising to his feet and pocketing his phone. He laid his hand on Milo's shoulder and squeezed gently. "Stay here, baby."

"No." Milo brushed us both off and raised his tear-stained face. His jaw was set stubbornly, his bright eyes blazing with determination. "I'm coming to help George."

"Me too." Like hell were they leaving me behind.

Everett looked like he might argue, but just sighed. "Fine. Get in the car. But neither of you are allowed anywhere near any danger."

We both agreed readily. Neither of us actually wanted to be hurt. There had to be other ways we could help George. I grabbed my jacket and a woolen hat and we left the remains of our dinners on the table and headed out to the car. Everett drove, with Milo in the passenger seat. Meanwhile, I called Knox.

"Hey, Danny," he greeted warmly.

"Knox, someone has taken George," I said, unable to hold back. "We're meeting at the Search and Rescue headquarters to make a plan. Do you think, with your nose, you could track his scent?"

"Who's George?" Knox's tone was businesslike now.

"The manager of the Children's Home."

"Damn." Muffled noises came down the line. "I'll see you there."

Everett parked outside the building and ushered us inside, staying behind us to watch our backs. We made a beeline for the bullpen, where the officers on duty—both those from the Sheriff's Department and the Search and Rescue team—were gathered.

Zander was at the center of the action. "Garrick will start coordinating a search team while we see what leads we can find at the Children's Home," he said, speaking loud enough for all to hear.

My heart squeezed. "Is someone already there?"

Surely they wouldn't have left the children unguarded.

"Hawk and Clay are with them," Zander replied, his gaze sharpening. "You shouldn't be here."

"I—"

He looked at something over my shoulder. "Nor should you."

I turned and spotted Knox's broad frame striding inside. My bear whimpered, begging me to throw myself into his arms and seek comfort, but I resisted the urge.

*Need mate.*

"No," I muttered to myself. "We have to help George."

We weren't in danger at the moment. He was.

"Danny called me." Knox stopped at my side, his hand brushing mine. My fingers twitched, desperate to curl around his.

Zander looked unimpressed. "You aren't police or search and rescue."

"But he has the best nose in town," I protested,

standing straight and raising my chin. "He's been doing everything he can to keep the community safe without any official support, and he has a better chance of finding George than we do."

Zander held my gaze for several seconds but I didn't back down. "Fine." He huffed and adjusted his hat. "Knox, come with me to the Children's Home."

"We're coming too." I took Milo's hand. "They'll be scared. They know us, and they're less likely to be intimidated if you have omegas with you."

Zander rolled his eyes. "Just get in the car."

Feeling a little smug, I followed Knox back through the door. Zander's police cruiser was parked on the roadside and the lights flashed as he unlocked it electronically. I got in the back and shuffled over to make room for Milo. The two alphas rode in the front.

We stopped a couple of blocks away and got out.

"I smell them." Knox lifted his nose and sniffed. "It was definitely the wolves, but I'll need something of George's if I'm going to trace his scent."

"In his bedroom," Milo said.

"He sleeps here?" Knox asked.

"Most nights."

We hastened inside. I lingered in the hall while Milo went to comfort the children and Knox disappeared into George's bedroom. He reappeared less than a minute later and went straight outside. I jogged behind him, but paused when he began to strip in the front yard. He shifted quickly, then barked and trotted off.

Jolted back into motion, I ran after him. He took off in one direction, then stopped and circled around. He shifted back.

"The scent dies here because he got into their car," he

said. "I'm going to run a perimeter around the township and see if it reappears anywhere."

I pursed my lips. "I can't imagine they'd let him out nearby, but I suppose it's worth a shot."

He grimaced. "I have to do something."

He shifted back and sprinted away. Something in my heart tugged as he got farther from me.

"No solid leads?"

I jumped, my hand flying to my chest. Slowly, I turned and found Zander behind me. "No, but he's still looking."

He nodded. "I'm returning to the office to find out what plan Garrick has come up with. Are you joining me or staying here with Milo?"

I hesitated. I should stay with Milo and the kids, but I wasn't sure whether I could stand being left out of the action. "I'll come with you."

I gathered Knox's clothes and took them with us as we drove back to headquarters. Zander led the way, and I sneaked a sniff of Knox's clothes, soothing myself with his scent.

Inside, Garrick was handing out assignments. I sat on a chair at the edge of the room and watched, knowing he wouldn't give me anything to do. At least I was here and would know the second anything happened.

My phone rang.

I flinched, having forgotten it was even in my pocket.

My heart skipped. It was George's number.

I answered quickly. "This is Danny."

"Danny, it's Knox. I have George. We're on Hampstead Road, just outside of town. We need someone to come and get us. Bring the doctor."

CHAPTER

# EIGHTEEN

K NOX
I stared at George, feeling utterly useless. He was sitting on the cold ground, hunched over and hugging his knees.

"Come quickly," I added, and ended the call.

I crouched beside George to study the wound on the left side of his head. Blood soaked his hair, and when I'd tried to examine it earlier, he'd screamed and tried to run away. Only the fact he'd tripped had kept him here for long enough for me to reassure him that I meant him no harm.

"George?" I tried to catch his gaze, but he was looking blankly into space. A shiver wracked his body. "Can I put my arms around you? You're freezing and we need to warm you up."

George wasn't a shifter. He had no internal heat regulation system, and all he was wearing was a short-sleeved shirt and slacks. He'd be hypothermic before long if he didn't let me help him.

When he failed to respond, I reached for him, but the instant my fingertips brushed his skin, he flinched.

"Shh." A sense of powerlessness threatened to over-whelm me. What could I do if he wouldn't accept my help? "It's all right. Please let me share my body heat."

He glanced at me, and the quick way his gaze flicked up and down my body reminded me that I was naked. Not a big deal for a shifter, but nudity tended to make humans uncomfortable.

"If I had clothes, I'd put them on." I sighed. "I'm not going to hurt you, or touch you inappropriately. The only omega I'm interested in is Danny. I have no desire to take advantage of you."

His eyebrows drew together, and he visibly forced himself to concentrate on my face. "Why do you think they targeted me?" he asked, his voice hollow. "Is it because I'm an omega? Or human?"

"I... don't know." I'd assume his being omega was key. The human part might have been a bonus since it would make him less able to resist them.

A sob caught in his throat. "They said they were going to use me as a fuck toy until I was broken and then throw me away."

My gut churned, and I had to swallow bile. The bitter taste lingered on my tongue and acid burned down the inside of my throat. What the fuck was wrong with those wolves?

"That isn't going to happen." I laid my hand on his arm more gently than I'd ever touched anyone in my life, and slowly rubbed, hoping the motion would soothe him. "You're safe now. If they want you, they'll have to go through me, and I won't go down easily."

He sniffled, and covered his mouth with one hand. "You promise?"

"Yeah." If it gave him peace, I'd fight for him. I was far

more comfortable with that than with trying to ease his tears. "George... why did they let you go?"

It had been bothering me since I'd come across him, but he'd been in such a state that I hadn't felt able to ask.

He made a derisive sound. "I fought. I don't think they expected me to. They were much stronger than me, and I didn't really stand a chance, but I think they worried that I'd delay them and they'd get caught. They said..." He worried his lower lip. "They said they'd be back to get me."

My grip tightened on his arm momentarily, but I loosened it before I scared him. "They will not take you."

I wouldn't allow it. No omega deserved to be so terrified that his scent soured the air for hundreds of yards around. Honestly, despicable as it was, I was amazed that the rogue wolves were even able to harm omegas at all. The stench of distressed omega was designed to send an alpha's protective instincts into overdrive.

An engine roared in the distance and I pricked my ears. "That's the Clan Alpha's car." I'd heard it several times before. "Do you hear that, George? Aaron is coming for you."

He blinked, tears spilling from the corners of his eyes. "But I'm not one of you."

I gritted my teeth. "Of course you are. You might not be a shifter, but I'd bet everything I have that Aaron Blackwood considers you part of his clan."

The car came into view and pulled over a short distance from us. The rear doors opened and Milo leaped from one side and Danny from the other. The two omegas rushed to George. I backed off so they could embrace him from each side.

George's tears fell harder, and he started to sob in earnest. Milo and Danny shushed him, and he seemed to draw comfort from their presence, clutching them tighter.

That sense of uselessness reasserted itself. I hadn't been able to help him. Not like they were.

Aaron got out of the driver's seat and circled around to stand in front of George. He rested one hand on the back of George's neck and exerted just enough pressure to let him know that he was there. Aaron's presence wouldn't calm George as it would a shifter, but he still had a reassuring air about him.

The passenger door opened and a polished older guy with the most impressive silver mustache I'd ever seen and wearing a suit, emerged. He moved briskly to George's side, carrying a briefcase—or perhaps a case of medical supplies. He noticed me staring and nodded politely before ushering Aaron aside and taking his place.

"How are you doing, George? It looks like you've got a nasty cut there." His voice was deep and even.

"Dr. Black." George fidgeted. He didn't seem sure what to focus on. "I don't think it needs stitches."

The older man—Dr. Black—tutted. "I'll be the judge of that. Let me get a better look."

While the doctor examined George's head, Milo kept one arm around the human, but Danny let him go and came over to join me. To my surprise, he hugged me.

"Thank you for finding George and being there when he needed you," he murmured, too softly for George to hear although no doubt the others all did.

I scoffed. "I hardly did anything. He was out in the open. Anyone could have found him. He got himself set free on his own, and all I did was make him nervous."

Danny frowned up at me, his arms still around my waist. "You were here in case he needed a protector. That counts for a lot."

I pressed my lips together and remained silent. I wasn't sure I agreed, but Danny and I were finally making progress in our relationship so I wasn't about to tell him so.

An icy breeze stirred the air, and I shivered. I wished I could hold Danny close and rest my cheek against his head, but he was currently touching me of his own volition and if I pushed him too far, he might pull back again.

"We'll need to take you back to the clinic for a proper assessment," the doctor was saying. "Is there anyone you'd like to call to have with you for that?"

George glanced at Milo, who nodded.

"I'll come," Milo said.

Dr. Black straightened. "Excellent. Let's get out of this cold."

He and Milo guided George into the front seat. I did a quick count and realized there weren't enough seats for all of us.

"I'll have to run back," I murmured to Danny. "I won't fit in the car."

He stiffened, and his jaw firmed. "I'll come with you."

"You don't have—"

"I'm coming." His tone dared me to argue.

I inclined my head. "Okay, then."

Danny turned to Aaron. "Dad, I'm going to run back with Knox. I'll see you later."

Aaron's dark gaze flicked from his son to me and back again. "Take care."

"We will." He didn't have to threaten me. If I ever let anything happen to Danny, I'd gladly punish myself.

Dr. Black and Milo got into the back seat of the car. Aaron opened the driver's door, looked back at us once more, and climbed in.

Danny pulled away from me, but twined our hands together. "Knox..."

I gripped his chin between my thumb and forefinger and tilted it up. "Mm?"

He hesitated, his teeth scraping over his lower lip. "Will you come back to my place tonight? I don't want to be alone."

# NINETEEN

D*ANNY*

My fingers trembled as I inserted the spare key into the lock. They were shaking so badly that I slipped and the key clattered onto the front porch.

Knox bent and picked it up. "Shh, baby. Let me." He unlocked the door and pushed it open. "Want me to go in first?"

I nodded. "Yes, please."

I hated to admit it, but George's abduction had terrified me. If he wasn't safe at the Children's Home in the center of town, then how could I possibly be safe alone in my house on the edge of the woods?

Knox stepped inside, waited for me to enter, closed the door quietly and snicked the lock back into place. Then he gestured for me to keep close behind him while he led the way through the house, moving from room to room. We made as little noise as possible, and I strained my ears, but all was silent.

Thank gods. No one was here.

Once we'd checked the whole house, Knox went to the

thermostat and turned it up higher. He switched on the kitchen lights and grabbed a mug from the cupboard.

"Want a snack and a hot chocolate?" he asked.

I fell for him a little then. Who wouldn't, when a man offered to care for someone so instinctively?

"Yes, please," I whispered, my heart so warm that I hardly noticed the chill in my fingers and toes.

He busied himself in the cabinets. "I'll get that for you. You just sit down and I'll be there in a moment."

My stomach fluttered. I could get used to this. I made my way to the sofa and pulled on the sweatpants hanging over the back of it, then sat.

Knox came over a short time after, carrying a blanket. He laid it over me and disappeared back into the kitchen again. My pulse raced, and adrenaline spiked as soon as he was out of sight.

You're safe, I reminded myself. The door is locked, and you're safe.

He emerged holding a mug topped with whipped cream and chocolate sprinkles and a small plate containing several pastries that he must have heated in the microwave. He set them on the coffee table and left again. Fear coursed through me. I wished he'd stop disappearing. My inner omega needed its alpha present in order to feel secure.

When he returned, he was carrying a second mug of hot chocolate, although this one smelled faintly of coffee too and didn't have any whipped cream or sprinkles on top. I scrunched my nose. It was the hot chocolate equivalent of a sludgy espresso.

"Sit beside me?" I asked, hating the note of pleading in my voice.

He did, but before he made himself comfortable, he grabbed my hot chocolate off the coffee table and offered it to me, along with a blackberry and honey pastry. I sipped the hot chocolate, ignoring the cream mustache that stuck to my upper lip, and took a bite of the pastry.

Yum. A delicious blend of sweetness and tartness, with a hint of spice.

"Want to talk about what just happened?" he asked, gazing at me steadily as he blew across the surface of his drink.

My cheeks heated. Suddenly, I wished he hadn't turned the lights on. "What do you mean?"

"Only a few seconds ago, you were so afraid that you were pumping out enough pheromones to affect me in the kitchen."

I pressed my lips together, shame spiraling through me. No, I didn't want to talk about it. Unfortunately, I got the impression that he wouldn't let this go easily.

"When you're near, I feel safe." I kept my eyes on my drink so I didn't have to see his reaction. "It terrifies me knowing that random alphas could decide to kidnap me at any moment. I can't fight one alpha, let alone several."

The admission shamed me further. I was a bear shifter. I was supposed to be strong.

Knox touched my knee, and when I didn't resist, he rested his hand there gently. "Keep in mind that they let George go because he put up a fight. He's human. I know you're more capable at defending yourself than he is."

My gut twisted. I wasn't sure that he was right. Perhaps, technically, I had the potential to be a stronger opponent than George, but not if I seized up, too scared to do anything to save myself.

"Drink," Knox prompted. "You need warmth and fuel."

I gulped down the hot chocolate, ignoring the sting in the back of my eyes.

"Even if you freeze, they won't have a chance to hurt

you." His raspy voice wrapped around me, as cozy as the blanket. "I won't let them. Just consider me your personal bodyguard."

*But I don't want you to get hurt either.*

I didn't say the words. I knew he'd take them as an affront to his strength.

"Thank you." I finished the drink and wiped the cream off my lip, sucking it from my finger. Knox's eyes darkened. "Can we watch a movie? Something sweet and fluffy."

He handed me the remote. "Whatever you like."

I searched through our streaming service until I found an adorable miniseries about two schoolboys falling in love. As I started it, I stuffed the rest of the pastry into my mouth and snuggled against Knox.

One of his arms came around my shoulders. I stiffened, expecting the constraint to make me nervous, but it didn't. Closing my eyes, I breathed in leather and pine, with traces of earth and the faint metallic bite of George's blood.

Even that didn't bother me, because Knox had protected George. Just like he'd protect me, if it came to it.

I tried to focus on the show's plotline, but more than once I became distracted by the play of shadows across Knox's face and the plushness of his lower lip.

I wanted to suck that lip into my mouth.

I wanted to taste him.

So I did.

Slowly—so he could stop me at any time—I stretched toward him until our lips touched. His short intake of breath rocked me to my core. I firmed the kiss, pressing myself against him, aligning the lengths of our bodies.

Knox tasted of chocolate, coffee, and comfort. I darted my tongue out, deepening the kiss, driven by an instinctive need to be close to him.

He groaned, and his palm curved around the side of my

neck, his grip tightening on the nape. He wasn't holding me hard, but his possessive grasp made me feel as though he was controlling every second of the exchange.

I loved it... until he pulled away.

"Danny." He nuzzled the crook of my neck, scenting me. "We can't do this now."

My stomach lurched. "B-but..."

I wanted him so badly. How could he be turning me away? Didn't he want me too?

"Hey. No. Whatever you're thinking, stop it." He gripped my jaw and angled my face toward him. "I want nothing more than to kiss you all night long, but I don't want you to wake up in the morning and regret it. You're feeling vulnerable right now. When we make things physical between us, it needs to be without any other emotions clouding the situation."

I gritted my back teeth together. I understood where he was coming from, but didn't he know that being close to him was the only way I felt safe? Or that my cock was hard as hell, which was a fucking miracle?

I hadn't been this turned on for months. Not since before Rex beat the crap out of me and was exiled from town. Honestly, I wasn't sure I'd ever been this turned on.

He dropped a gentle kiss on the tip of my nose. "How about we go to bed and snuggle?"

Bed? But hadn't he said...?

"Just to sleep." He loosened his grip on me. "I want to hold you. Nothing more, I promise."

I relaxed. Of course that was all he wanted. I considered the suggestion for a long moment. It was scary. It would mean making myself more vulnerable with him than I'd been with anyone for a long time. Sleeping beside someone required a lot of trust.

But he'd saved George.

He was trying to protect me from my own impulsive behavior.

Surely, I could trust him enough for this.

I took a deep breath and nodded. "Okay."

CHAPTER

# TWENTY

K*NOX*

I woke with my mate in my arms. Burrowing my face into his hair, I inhaled his scent and sank into the soft embrace of the mattress. He smelled of warmth, honey, sleepy man... and me. It was a combination I could get used to, if he'd let me.

I raised my head and looked around. It was no longer completely dark, so morning must be upon us. Unfortunately, that meant I had to make a decision, and I wasn't sure what to do. Should I stay in bed with Danny or sneak out before he woke up and panicked?

Last night he'd been stressed, and his instincts had overridden his fear of me. In the cold light of day, and with several hours of rest up his sleeve, he'd be in a clearer mindset. There was every chance he'd realize that we'd made a mistake and he didn't truly want me here.

But if I left while he was asleep and he didn't wake up with regrets, then he'd be upset with me, and rightfully so. Mates shouldn't slink away in the morning like they're ashamed. They should stand by each other's sides and face the future together.

110

Damn it. This wasn't helping.

And to think, I'd once believed that finding a mate would be the hard part, and after that, everything would fall nicely into place.

Ha.

I dithered, going back and forth before finally deciding to get out of bed but stay in the house. That way, when he woke, he wouldn't be forced to endure me holding him if he didn't want to, but he wouldn't feel abandoned either.

Moving slowly, I disentangled myself from him and eased from the bed, being careful not to disturb him. When I was free, I tiptoed out of the room, closed the door, and went to the bathroom to wash up.

After a shower, I felt better, but I didn't have anything to wear. I'd probably find something belonging to one of Danny's brothers if I rummaged through the drawers, but I didn't want to invade his privacy like that, so I tied a towel around my waist instead.

I headed to the kitchen, started the coffee brewing, and examined the contents of the cupboards. I considered making a full cooked breakfast, but after Danny's shock yesterday, he needed something nourishing, so I prepared a healthy tray of cut fruit drizzled with honey, granola, and yogurt.

By the time he emerged from the bedroom, the tray was laid on the dining table, along with a cup of coffee for each of us, prepared to our preferences.

"What's this?" he asked, rubbing his tired eyes.

"Breakfast." I pulled out one of the chairs for him and gestured for him to sit. "Coffee, just how you like it, and a nice healthy breakfast to get us off to a good start for the day."

A shy smile crept over his face and his gaze skimmed

my naked chest before he looked away. "This looks really nice. Thank you."

"You're welcome." If I had my way, he'd get used to being spoiled every day.

Danny sat, and we ate breakfast together in peaceful silence. When we were done, he excused himself to shower and get dressed while I cleared away the dirty dishes.

"Can we visit George?"

I glanced toward the hall doorway, where Danny was now standing. "Of course."

It would be good to check on the little omega and see how he was doing after a night of rest. Likely, the reality of what had happened would finally have sunk in. He might be jittery and nervous, in which case, the company of another adult omega would help.

"Would you like to walk down?" I asked. "It's sunny outside. I doubt it's very warm, but some fresh air might do us good."

"Yeah, that's fine. Just let me grab my jacket and a change of clothes for you." He disappeared down the hall and returned a moment later, already zipping up his puffer jacket. He passed me a bundle of clothes and I took it to the bathroom and tugged on the pair of sweatpants, T-shirt, and jacket he'd provided me with. They were slightly too large, but they'd do.

I joined Danny and waited for him to precede me through the front door, then locked it behind us and fell into step beside him. As we walked, his fingers brushed mine, and a jolt of electricity rippled through me. I curled my hand away, unsure whether the contact would make him uncomfortable, but then he slid his hand into mine and gripped it tightly.

My heart swelled. Inside, my wolf howled with joy. Our

mate had willingly taken our hand. We were getting closer to bonding.

We strolled down the main street, past the bakery, the hardware store, and the police station until the children's home came into view. I was pleased to see a police officer stationed out the front. Zander was clearly taking the threat to its inhabitants' safety seriously.

The officer straightened as we approached. He nodded to Danny. "Good morning." His gaze traveled to me and grew suspicious. "How can I help you both?"

"We're here to see George." Danny's grasp of my hand tightened infinitesimally. "Is that okay?"

The officer relaxed. "I don't see any harm in that, but I'll have to check whether he wants to talk to the two of you first." He turned to me. "What's your name again, wolf?"

Danny started to scowl, but I didn't take offense. The cop was just doing his job.

"Knox Kingston. Tell George it's the guy who found him last night."

The cop dipped his head in acknowledgment. "I'll do that. Just wait a moment. And by the way, thank you for what you did yesterday. I know we all appreciate it."

He raised his radio to his mouth and spoke into it quietly, relaying our message. A few seconds later, a response came through.

"You can go in," he said.

"Thanks." Danny released my hand and, when the cops stepped aside, bustled into the house.

I paused before following him. "Is there someone guarding the Omega House?"

They were vulnerable too. Just because the rogue wolves had opted to attack the Children's Home once didn't mean it would be the target of choice a second time.

"They are." A hint of respect gleamed in the cop's eyes. "Don't worry, we protect our own."

"Good." I could only hope that one day I would be counted amongst that number.

I entered the house and followed the sound of voices to a cozy living room. Danny sat on an armchair while George was huddled on the sofa with a child tucked under each arm—a little blond boy on his left and a pretty dark-skinned girl on his right. A brief sniff identified them as a squirrel shifter and a bear shifter, respectively.

Danny and George seemed to be sharing an intense conversation, so I kept my distance, not wanting to intrude. I was waiting for an opening to ask how George was doing, but before the chance arose, footsteps padded up the hall behind me. I didn't turn, able to identify the newcomer by scent.

Garrick.

"Zander called me," he murmured, coming to a stop a few feet behind me. "He told me I could find you here."

"And why did you want to find me?" I asked, keeping my eyes on Danny.

Garrick chuckled. "Fair question. Look, I know we've all been a bit wary of you, but you really proved yourself last night. If you hadn't taken the initiative, there's no saying how long George might've been outside before someone found him."

I shrugged. "You would have found him eventually. I just got there first."

"Because you're good." Garrick shifted his weight from one foot to the other, his clothes rustling as he moved. "We'd like to have you on the search and rescue team on a probationary basis, if you're interested."

My heart stuttered. I didn't know what to say. On the

one hand, the job showed a level of acceptance that I'd been looking for, and it would mean cash. On the other hand... Well, I couldn't help but feel like that acceptance was either conditional or against their better judgment, and I didn't know what to make of that.

# TWENTY-ONE

**D**ANNY

I'd been keeping one ear on my conversation with George and the other on Knox's with Garrick. As soon as I heard Garrick offer Knox a job, I could no longer focus on George. My heart lifted and I jumped to my feet and ran over to them.

"Knox would be perfect for that," I exclaimed. I beamed at my brother, and then at my mate. "You have to say yes. It's just right for you."

Knox's eyebrows drew together and a groove formed between them. He didn't look nearly as thrilled as I'd have expected. I scanned his face, taking in his obvious reluctance.

I didn't understand. He'd been trying to get a job and failing. Surely this offer should be good news—especially since it played so well to his strengths and experience.

Knox met my gaze. His deep, dark eyes burned into mine, as if looking right down into the very core of who I was. I shivered.

His lips curved slightly. "I'll take the job."

"Great." Garrick clapped him on the shoulder. "You can

start tomorrow. Come in later today to fill out the paperwork."

"Will do." Knox hesitated, then added, "Let me know if you need more muscle protecting the Children's Home, the Omega House, or anyone else who's vulnerable in the community."

Garrick nodded. "I will, but I think we've got it covered at the moment." He winked at me, then turned away. "I better get back to the office."

He left. I glanced over at George, knowing I should rejoin him, but I couldn't help feeling that Knox needed me. I took his hand and drew him down the hall and into the bathroom.

"Why don't you seem pleased about the job?" I asked, nibbling on my lower lip.

"I am." His tone didn't go far in making me buy his story.

I huffed. "Then why the long face?"

He opened his mouth, and judging from his expression, it seemed like he was about to shut me down, but then he thought better of it.

"What is it?" I asked softly. "You can tell me anything."

He paced to the other end of the room and back, dragging his palm down his face. "It's just that, sure, Garrick offered me a job, but I know neither he nor anyone else actually wants me here. They're tolerating me because I'm useful and because you're pushing them to, but that doesn't change the reality."

My heart dropped and my face fell. Guilt squirmed in the pit of my gut.

My mate believed himself to be unwanted, and I hadn't helped. My rejection had only turned him into more of an outcast.

"No. No, no, no." Tears welled in my eyes. "That's not

how it is. No one wants you to leave. No one dislikes you. I'm really sorry that things have been hard for you, but I'm really glad that you've stuck around and weathered it for me." My chest tightened and emotion clogged my throat, making it difficult to speak.

Knox grunted, and his dark gaze followed me. Now it was my turn to pace, as I wondered how I'd let things get this bad.

"No one wants you gone," I promised. "I hate that my fear has done this to you, but once people see us getting closer, they'll warm up to you. It will all be okay."

"Maybe." He didn't look like he believed it.

I supposed I'd just have to prove it to him. Hopefully, the job would help too. Seeing him contribute to the community could only be a good thing for the rest of the clan.

"What can I do?" I felt useless. But wasn't that always the problem? I was weak. Milo would know what to say to make him feel better. Any of my brothers would have a practical solution. I just... dithered.

"Nothing." His expression closed off. "Like you said, it will be fine."

"But..."

Knox forced a smile, but it didn't reach his eyes. "So." He slid his hands into his pockets and relaxed his stance. "It's only a week until Christmas now. What would you be doing to celebrate?"

I chewed on the corner of my thumbnail, unsure whether to persist or let him change the subject. In the end, I was too cowardly to push. "My family will spend the day together. We always use the holidays to bond and reconnect before the New Year."

"Oh."

He didn't say whether he had plans, and I didn't ask.

Did he have anyone out there who cared for him? I had no idea. Would he be alone for the holidays?

The possibility made me unaccountably sad. Perhaps I should invite him to our Christmas festivities. But surely that would be an indication that I was ready to acknowledge him as my mate, and I wasn't yet.

I could hardly abandon him at such a time though, could I?

# CHAPTER
# TWENTY-TWO

K*NOX*

Tipping back the last of a glass of whiskey, I murmured, "Merry Christmas to me."

The alcohol burned down my throat, and I closed my eyes and listened to Mariah Carey serenading me through the radio. Honestly, Christmas music drove me fucking crazy, but I couldn't bring myself to turn it off.

When the sharp taste of whiskey began to fade from my mouth, I blinked my eyes open and gazed out the window of my little cabin. Snow was falling and a thin layer had already settled on the ground. Despite the cold outside here, it was warm in my temporary home. I'd lit the fire and since the space was so small, it was easy to keep it cozy.

What was less easy was fighting off the loneliness that had been knocking on the edge of my subconscious all day. I hadn't seen anyone. I hadn't gotten a tree or bothered to decorate. There was no point. Danny was busy with his family, and there was no one else who was likely to drop by.

Yuri and Li had invited me to join their family for Christmas dinner, but I didn't know them well, and I didn't want to intrude. I would have felt too awkward, like a cuckoo in their nest. Better to keep to myself. Perhaps I was miserable, but at least no one else was.

I clunked my empty glass onto the stool beside the armchair and inhaled deeply, drawing the scent of burning wood and cinnamon into my lungs.

Okay, so perhaps I hadn't been entirely unsentimental. I'd heated a slice of the apple pie that Danny had given me and recalled his shy expression as he'd offered it to me. At least if I didn't have him, I still had something he'd made me.

What would he be doing right now?

I knew he'd been having lunch with his family, but had that finished or was he still with them?

He was probably with them. I got the feeling his family were like those strangely happy ones featured in Hallmark movies. They probably spent every waking minute together and never got tired of each other.

I heard knuckles rap on the front door. I started and sat up quickly, caught off guard. I hadn't heard anyone approach. Although I couldn't say I'd been paying too much attention. I was too busy wallowing.

Not to mention the fact I'd had a couple of drinks. That in itself was enough to dull my senses. Still, no one should have been able to get the drop on me. I sniffed and almost groaned at the delicious combination of sugar and honey with a hint of bourbon.

Danny.

I got up, strode to the door, unlocked it and opened it. He smiled up at me, snowflakes melting on the tips of his hair, his cheeks flushed from the cold. My stomach flipped over. Damn, he was beautiful.

"What are you doing here?" I asked.

He offered me a small square container, which I hadn't noticed he was holding. I took it from him. "I'm here to spend the afternoon with you."

I cocked my head. "I thought you were doing a family thing."

He flashed me his teeth. "That's finished now, and I want to spend time with my mate."

*Mate.*

My wolf growled its approval. My heart skipped, and I tried to read the intention behind his words in his eyes.

"Your mate? Does that mean we're acknowledging that we're mates now?"

Danny rubbed his lips together and looked down at his hands. "No one ever denied it, but I was scared, and it took me a while to work past my fear. Can I come in?"

I hesitated.

"Unless..." His face crumpled. "You don't want me here?"

"No," I hurried to say. "It's not that. It's just... Well, my place isn't going to be very impressive after spending Christmas morning and most of the day with your family in that nice big house your parents have."

Danny rolled his eyes. "I'm not judging you based on where you live and how much you decorated. I promise."

"Okay then." I stepped aside. "Come in."

I glanced down at the container he'd given me. "What's in here?"

"Bourbon balls. I know you said you tend to like savory things more than sweet things and this gives you a little bit of both. It shouldn't be too sweet for you, but my specialty is sweet things so I had to work with the skills I have."

Warmth unfurled within me. "I'm sure I'll love them. Thank you."

He bounced on the balls of his feet. "If you don't just let me know, and next time I'll try something different."

He was nervous. It eased something inside of me. I

pressed myself against the wall as he entered, and then closed the door and locked it behind him. I probably didn't need to be as vigilant with locks here as I'd been in other places but with my mate on the premises, I wasn't taking any chances.

I popped open the lid of the container and plucked out one of the bourbon balls, Pinching it between my thumb and forefinger. I bit into it, and flavor exploded in my mouth. So good. A little sweet, very rich, but somehow without going over the edge into being too much.

"Amazing," I told him. "Just like I knew they would be."

He blushed, drawing attention to a spattering of freckles across his nose. Adorable.

I gestured toward the sofa. "Want to sit? I can get you a drink. Coffee?"

He hesitated. "Do you have hot chocolate?"

"I do. A special chili chocolate blend. Less sweet than usual, is that okay?" I knew his tastes ran sweeter than mine.

"Sounds perfect." He smiled and reached into his pocket. "I have something for you."

My pulse skipped. A gift? I couldn't remember the last time anyone gave me a gift. My dad sure as hell had never bothered.

I supposed it would have been Mom. A gentle ache started in my chest. No matter how much time passed since I'd lost her, the grief never went away. It just faded into the background some days, only to emerge stronger on others.

"You didn't have to do that," I said.

"I know." He pulled out a small package wrapped in black tissue paper. "I wanted to. I want you to know how much your patience means to me, and that I do want to work toward having a future together."

I placed the bourbon balls on the coffee table and took

the tissue-wrapped item from him, being as gentle as I knew how to be. Hopefully whatever was inside wasn't too delicate because I was better at breaking things than keeping them safe.

I glanced at Danny's face to check that he wanted me to open it, and when he nodded, I peeled off a small black sticker holding two pieces of the paper together. I unwrapped the package to reveal a thin chain with a small metal bear charm hanging from it.

"I noticed that you wear a necklace." He waved his hand toward the leather strap around my neck. "So I was hoping that meant you're open to other jewelry, but don't feel like you have to put it on. It's just to remind you of me and it's kind of a promise to work on building our relationship."

"It's perfect." I leaned over and kissed his cheek. "Thank you, Danny. I couldn't have asked for anything better."

Now I wished I'd gotten him something more meaningful.

"Would you like me to do it up for you?" he asked, picking at the skin beside his thumbnail.

"Only if you stop hurting yourself," I said, indicating his red thumb.

He laughed. "Nervous habit. Sorry."

I didn't like the fact he was nervous around me, but at least he was here. That's more than I'd expected. I lowered my head and turned so he could loop the chain around my neck and fasten the clasp. The metal felt warm as it settled against my skin, not cold as I'd expected.

He finished fussing and moved back. "There."

"I, uh, got you something too."

"You did?" He looked pleased.

"Of course. I only have one mate." There was no one else I'd even consider buying a gift for at the moment.

Although I supposed that might explain why my offering left something to be desired compared to his. I didn't have much experience with choosing gifts. "Hold on."

I hurried into the bedroom, collected the gift-wrapped box, and took it out to him. His eyes widened, and his quick pulse betrayed his excitement. I passed him the box, and he sat on the sofa and tore the paper off carefully so as not to damage anything underneath.

He flashed his pearly teeth. "It's a set of new pastry brushes."

I inhaled silently, hoping to detect whether or not he was disappointed. I didn't note anything to that effect. "I know it's not very romantic, but Skye said you wanted some."

His coworker was one of the few people who'd always been welcoming toward me, and she'd been happy to help me think of a gift for Danny.

"I have." He studied the front of the box. "These are my favorite brand too."

I touched the side of my nose. Thank you, Skye.

"I love them." He placed the box on the sofa and stretched onto his toes to kiss my cheek. My heart skipped, and my wolf stirred beneath the surface. Danny smelled of everything that was good about the world, and I could bask in his scent all day.

"Will you play with me?" he asked.

I frowned. "What do you mean?"

He gestured out the window, where it was still snowing. "In the snow. In our other forms."

Butterflies swooped inside me. "Absolutely. Now?"

He nodded.

Not needing any further encouragement, I stripped off my clothes and went back through the process of unlocking the door and opening it. Once outside, I looked over my shoulder just in time to see Danny toss his shirt aside.

Grinning, I took a few steps forward as my shift came over me. Fur rippled over my skin and I shrank lower to the ground, planting my paws on the soft snow.

There was a snuffling behind me and I spun around, tail wagging as Danny's grizzly pawed at the snow. I circled around him, yipping excitedly. He scooped up snow—poorly—with one paw and sprayed me with it. The icy crystals sprinkled my muzzle and I tried to swipe them up with my tongue.

Danny straightened to his full height, and I lunged forward, ready to pounce on him, but remembered at the last minute that doing so might scare him, so I nipped at his ankles and rolled onto my back in front of him, showing him my belly.

It went against every alpha instinct I possessed, but he needed to see that I wasn't a threat.

He nuzzled my belly, working his way up to my throat, and then, with playful eyes, he darted away. I took off after him, chasing him across the street, my paws wet and cold but my heart warmer than ever.

Together, we frolicked in the snow until the chill had soaked through our fur and to our bones, then we returned inside and huddled in front of the fire. I kept my arm around him, hardly able to believe the turn this day had taken.

Danny met my eyes. "You should come for supper at my parents' house tonight."

My pulse leaped. "Yeah?"

He pouted. "Please."

Gods, he was irresistible like that.

"All right." I cleared my throat. "I'll come."

I just hoped they wouldn't be unhappy to see me there.

# TWENTY-THREE

**D**ANNY

As I walked hand-in-hand with Knox into my parents' dining room, everyone turned toward us, stunned. Momma was the first one to get over her shock. She hurried over to us, the reindeer on her awful Christmas sweater glittering beneath the bright lights.

"Knox, it's so good to have you here." She took his hand and squeezed it. "Thank you for coming, and Merry Christmas to you."

Knox tipped his head respectfully. "Merry Christmas to you too, Melinda. I appreciate you having me." He offered her the bottle of mulled wine he'd insisted on bringing as a hostess gift. "Here. I hope you like this. I don't know much about wine."

Momma took the bottle and rotated it to read the label. "I'm sure it'll be lovely. Why don't I heat this while you find a seat? Knox, I don't know how much Danny has told you, but we have a Christmas tradition that's a little like Thanksgiving. We'll be doing that soon."

Knox nodded as if he knew what she was talking about. He didn't. I'd never mentioned it, too worried that he'd refuse if he knew that he was going to be put on the spot. Perhaps that made me a bad mate, but I'd felt so terrible when I'd realized how lonely he must have been today and I'd needed him to come with me so I could make up for it.

Momma patted his shoulder and headed off with the wine.

"Good evening, Knox," Dad said, joining us. The two men shook hands. I looked from one to the other. While Dad was larger and had a more commanding presence, there was something about Knox that just screamed that he was dangerous.

"Good evening, Alpha." Knox bared his neck, showing his submission. The gesture came easily, as if he'd spent a lifetime doing it, and I couldn't help wondering where he'd come from before he'd arrived here. Had he always been a loner, or had he once belonged to a pack?

He must have been part of a pack at one point, or at least had parents. Where were they now?

"Garrick says you're a real asset to the Search and Rescue team," Dad said, gesturing toward my brother, who was locked in an intense conversation with Zander. I kept an eye on them for a few seconds. Were they discussing work at the dinner table? Because I couldn't think of any other reason they'd look so serious.

"I'm enjoying it," Knox replied, his scent staying clean, proving his honesty. Then again, I wasn't surprised. I'd known the job would be a good fit, and I got the impression that Knox was someone who liked to be busy—and preferably, useful.

"That's good." Dad pointed to a pair of seats at the nearest end of the table, opposite Milo and Everett. "Why don't you two sit there?"

"Yes, Alpha." Knox took my elbow and guided me into the seat.

Momma returned with the mulled wine in a jug and placed it on the table, along with the leftovers from earlier. We'd all eaten well at lunch, so I wasn't particularly hungry, but I'd worked up a bit of an appetite after playing with Knox earlier.

Dad sat at the head of the table, nearest to Garrick and Zander, and Momma claimed the chair to his right.

"For those of you who don't know the drill, think of this as similar to Thanksgiving," Momma said. "I want to hear one thing that each of you are happy about and one thing you're grateful for right now. I'll go first. I'm grateful to have all of my babies in one place, and I'm happy to see our family growing."

Beside me, Knox made a noise in the back of his throat. I grabbed his hand beneath the table.

Garrick went next, followed by Zander, Everett, and Milo.

When it was my turn, I looked around the table and smiled. "I'm grateful for family, and I'm happy to be here with all of you."

Knox stiffened, clearly nervous. "I'm, uh, grateful to you all for letting me join you, and I'm happy to have met Danny."

Aww.

My heart contracted, and emotion twisted in my gut. He was so sweet, and when I chanced a look at him, his eyes were sincere. But I wasn't sure that I actually deserved him. Not after how I'd pushed him away and left him to struggle on his own. Even now, I didn't fully trust him, no matter how badly I wanted to.

We completed the circle and began to eat. Knox relaxed beside me and I poured a glass of mulled wine for each of us. He served me one of the blackberry pastries that hadn't been eaten earlier with a dollop of cream.

My bear preened. Our mate was caring for us.

Across the table, Milo asked about our afternoon. I told him about the beautiful new pastry brush set that Knox had given me, and then showed him the necklace around Knox's neck. Something inside me thrilled at the sign of ownership over him. He'd let me adorn his body. Surely that meant I had some kind of claim to him?

Perhaps it wasn't fair to be so pleased about that when he didn't have the same visual claim over me, but my bear remained smug despite that.

*Our mate*, he insisted. *Ours.*

I sighed internally. *I know, buddy. But we're not ready for more yet.*

My mind wandered as I sipped the rich, dark mulled wine, enjoying the way it warmed me from the inside out. But just as I was about to tune into a conversation Everett and Knox were having, I heard something farther up the table that almost stopped my heart.

"...Rex," Garrick muttered.

I froze and turned toward him slowly. Everyone fell silent, perhaps scenting the fear and anger that emanated from me.

"We don't mention that name here," I growled, almost animalistic. "He's off-limits."

Garrick grimaced. "I'm sorry, Danny. You're right. I won't do it again."

I nodded and focused on my food, stabbing a piece of blackberry and forking it into my mouth. I could feel Knox's eyes on me and knew he was curious, but I was in no mood to explain. I was sure he already knew a little, and I was too ashamed to tell him more unless it couldn't be avoided.

"What are your Christmas traditions?" I asked him, in an effort to get his mind off the subject of my ex.

He shrugged. "I don't have any."

"No?" That couldn't be right. Everyone had holiday traditions, even if they didn't like them.

Knox side-eyed me. "My family is a long story. Let's just say I've never had the typical Christmas experience."

"Oh." My heart ached for him, and I wished even harder that I'd been brave enough to invite him for the whole day. Next year, I'd make sure he came. "If you ever want to talk about your family, I'm here to listen."

The corners of his mouth firmed. "Maybe another time. When we're alone."

Crap. Of course he didn't want to talk where my nosy family would be able to hear every word. I shook my head, disgusted with myself. I'd been a terrible mate, rejecting him at every turn and leaving him to wallow in his loneliness on a day that was supposed to be joyous. Now I couldn't even offer help the right way.

I focused on sipping my wine, hoping he wouldn't smell my inner turmoil. What did I really know about Knox? He hadn't mentioned his family to me, and I hadn't asked. I didn't even know whether he had siblings or if his parents were still alive. He'd been trying so hard to win me over, and I'd done the bare minimum in return.

*Do better, Danny.*

We kept to light subjects for the rest of the meal, and when Everett and Milo left, I said my good nights as well. Momma hugged me and then Knox, ignoring the tension in his muscles. If he'd seemed bothered by the embrace, I'd have stopped it, but I think he was just surprised. Maybe physical affection wasn't common wherever he'd grown up.

My parents ushered us out the door, but not before Momma extracted a promise from Knox to come by again soon.

Once outside, he exhaled sharply.

"You okay?" I asked.

"Fine." He waved toward my house. "I'll walk you home."

"You don't have to do that," I protested. It was literally right there. I could be in the door in less than a minute if I wanted.

He gave me a look that said he wasn't taking no for an answer. I rolled my eyes, but inside, my stomach swooped and I was a little giddy that he felt so protective of me.

He escorted me to my front door and hovered while I unlocked it.

"Will you tell me about him sometime?" he asked cautiously.

The question startled me. I flinched but hid it—hopefully before he noticed my reaction.

I pursed my lips. He could only mean one person. I was tempted to tell him everything, but surely he'd look at me differently when he realized that I was damaged goods.

"I-I can't," I stammered, stumbling through the doorway into the house. He caught my shoulder and steadied me. "One day, maybe, but not right now. Please."

He stiffened for a moment, his muscles coiled, but then relaxed again. I breathed a sigh of relief, instinctively knowing that he was about to let me off the hook.

I couldn't avoid telling him the truth forever, but at least I'd bought myself some time. I just wish I knew how long it would last.

# CHAPTER
# TWENTY-FOUR

*KNOX*

"So, what do we tell human law enforcement about how we track their missing people?" I asked Yuri as we drove toward a trailhead to search for a pair of missing hikers who had apparently decided that a midwinter hike would be the perfect way to see out the end of the year.

"Bloodhounds," Yuri explained, switching on his turn signal and executing a turn onto a pot-holed gravel road.

"But they see us sometimes," I pointed out. "Surely they realize we don't have dogs with us."

Yuri shrugged. "Could be magic. I don't know. If you're that curious, ask Garrick."

"Maybe later."

He pulled into a parking area and turned off the car. Garrick and Everett stopped behind us. We didn't have the whole team here because it should be a relatively simple search job, although I knew they were on call if we needed them.

I opened the passenger door and got out, stretching my cramped arms above my head. Gods, I hated being stuck in a car. Motorcycles were so much better. The wind in my face, the smell of fresh air and hot asphalt. Nothing could beat it.

Well, nothing other than Danny.

Garrick dumped a plastic tub on the ground for us to store our clothes in. "Everett and Knox, you're our best trackers. I want you to shift. Yuri and I will stay on foot. That way, when we find them, we can engage the hikers while you disappear into the woods and circle back around."

"Got it." I stripped off my clothes and chucked them into the tub, not bothering to fold them. I left my heavy boots beside the tub, not wanting to get our clothes muddy.

I shifted and jogged around the edge of the parking area, noting scents and searching for anything of concern. There didn't seem to be any reason to worry so I returned to Garrick and Yuri. Everett was sitting on his haunches, towering over me in his bear form, although I liked to think I could take him if I had to.

Yuri held out a pale blue and white blouse and a pair of khaki shorts. "You can get their scents from these. The local ranger retrieved them from the hikers' vehicle."

I sniffed the blouse, inhaling hints of chamomile and jasmine. The shorts had a more musky scent, with traces of salt from sweat. I backed off, giving Everett space to smell them, and retraced my footsteps around the parking area. I was certain I recognized that combination of chamomile and jasmine.

When I found the scent, I barked to get the others' attention. Everett lumbered over and skimmed his nose across the dirt. He nodded and jerked his nose toward the trail, indicating for me to lead the way.

My stomach flipped. I hadn't been trusted to take the lead yet—not that it particularly mattered, since we worked as a team—but it felt good to be trusted. I waited for Yuri and Garrick to join us and followed the scent trail into the woods.

We meandered along for a while, until we reached an area where the scent diverged from the marked trail. They must have either lost the trail or intentionally left it.

It was rougher going as we traveled through the untouched part of the woods. I pushed through the brush and circled trees, the others close behind. At least Everett and I were having an easier time of it than Yuri and Garrick.

We reached a large rock and I veered to the right, following the faint traces of chamomile and jasmine, but Everett growled and trotted the other way. I cocked my head, uncertain what he was doing, but when I headed toward him, I realized the musky male scent had gone left.

I shifted back. "They separated."

Garrick scowled. "Great. Why do they always do that? Have they not seen any horror movies?"

Yuri laughed. "This isn't a horror movie. If it were, we'd be the bad guys."

The man had a point. Humans were notoriously suspicious of anything they didn't understand, and there were enough gory werewolf films to prove that we weren't an exception.

"Yuri, stick with Knox and follow the right trail," Garrick said, ignoring him and glancing at his watch. "Everett and I will go left. Turn around if you haven't found anything in the next two hours and we can make a new plan."

I returned to my wolf form and followed the weak scent of chamomile. Five minutes passed. Then ten. Yuri began chatting out loud despite the fact I was unable to reply. He must not like the silence.

"It's good to see Danny starting to come out of his shell

again," he said, circling around a large root system that I'd padded over without a second thought. "I think you're good for him. He wasn't the same after Rex... well, after Rex. He used to be so sassy. But he really withdrew into himself. We all wanted to help, but none of us knew how to."

My hackles rose. I sniffed the air, detecting the faint undertone of Yuri's anger. I didn't respond though, wanting to know more about Rex and what had happened between him and Danny. I ignored the kernel of guilt festering inside me, reminding me that Danny had yet to share any of this with me.

I sniffed a patch of dirt and focused on finding our missing female hiker.

"Shifters heal quickly but it was still obvious he'd been hurt." Yuri shook his head, grumbling words that made no sense. "We should have noticed that something was wrong. Fuck..."

I couldn't take it anymore. I couldn't continue listening and pretend that all this was familiar to me. It wasn't right. I had to let Danny tell me what he wanted to in his own time. I halted and turned toward Yuri, then shifted onto two legs.

"Please don't say anything more." I kept my tone soft so he would know that I wasn't angry with him. "Danny and I haven't had this conversation yet, and I think he deserves to be the one who tells me however much he wants to."

Yuri paled. "Shit, man. I'm so sorry. I didn't realize." He groaned and closed his eyes. "Gods, he is going to kick my ass for this."

"Don't worry." I held my hands up conciliatorily, "I won't mention it. Just don't tell me anything else."

"I won't."

I shifted back to my wolf form and started up the trail. Yuri stayed close behind me, although he didn't talk anymore, probably worried about giving away more secrets.

Another hundred yards down the trail, the hiker veered into the woods. I moved my head in that direction to let Yuri know, then I followed it, winding between trees and ducking around bushes. The scent grew stronger, meaning that it was either more recent or that the source was nearby. I was inclined to think both might be the case.

Sure enough, the rhythmic thud of a heartbeat sounded up ahead. I peered through the woods, searching for a figure. When I spotted her, I nudged Yuri in that direction. I waited until it was obvious he'd seen her too and then left him to escort her back while I went to find Everett and Garrick.

By the time I tracked them down, Garrick was walking back toward the vehicles with his arm around a limping guy in his mid-twenties. Everett was nowhere to be seen, so I assumed he had done the same as me and gotten out of sight of the humans. I barked softly to let Garrick know I was there and dashed away, following Everett back out of the woods.

I found him in the parking area, already dressed. I pulled on my clothes and leaned against the car.

"Did you hear what happened?" I asked him.

He grunted, his face twisted with disapproval. "Apparently they deliberately went off the trail, intending to use a shortcut, but then got lost. They made the brilliant decision to separate when they reached the rock because they thought they could use it as a landmark to return to. The man went to look for a phone signal, while the woman was searching for shelter. When it was time to meet at the rock, neither of them could find it again."

"Ugh." Now I understood his annoyance. Some people just couldn't seem to make good decisions. Everything looked the goddamn same in the woods. They shouldn't rely on their ability to navigate them without help.

"Yeah. Don't worry, I've called the ranger, and he'll be here soon; then the hikers will be his problem."

That was something, at least.

"Paramedics, too?" I asked. "It looks like that guy had hurt his ankle."

"I told the ranger he might need medical attention but that it didn't look serious." Everett crossed his arms. "I'm not sure whether he'll bring someone or not."

Our question was answered less than ten minutes later when the ranger appeared, alone in a green Jeep. He parked and greeted us with a friendly smile.

"There's always someone, isn't there?" he asked, very nonchalant about the whole thing. "Don't worry, boys, I've had first-aid training and I brought food and water. I'll have them all sorted in no time."

I was glad to hear it. I was more than ready to leave when Garrick and Yuri emerged from the woods with the two hikers in tow. We handed them off into the ranger's care, and Yuri and I started the drive back to Grizzly Ridge while Garrick did whatever official business he needed to close out the case.

When we arrived at the search and rescue station, Danny came rushing out, carrying a pair of coffees and a brown paper bag.

"A double espresso for Knox, and a cappuccino for Yuri," he said, thrusting the take-out cups into our hands. "Did you find everyone safely?"

"Yeah. They were fine." I smiled at him. "Thanks for the coffee."

He beamed, his cheeks flushing with pleasure. "You're welcome. There are cheese and bacon croissants in the bag as well. I thought you might need a snack."

My heart warmed. "That was very thoughtful of you."

I tipped back the espresso, not bothering to savor the bitter taste as it drained down my throat, giving me an instant burst of energy.

Danny offered me the paper bag. I took it, and with his hand free, he touched my elbow and took me aside, putting a little space between us and Yuri.

"There's a midnight run today to celebrate New Year's Eve. Will you come?"

# CHAPTER
# TWENTY-FIVE

*DANNY*

I gazed at the reflection in my parents' bathroom mirror, wondering if Knox would like what he saw. I'd dressed in my best dark wash jeans with a salmon-colored shirt that set off my complexion nicely. My hair was styled and I'd shaved in more than one place.

Anxiety curled in my gut. I hadn't worn this shirt since before I'd started dating Rex. He hadn't liked it. He'd said that the color was too feminine and that I was a bear shifter and shouldn't like girly things.

It had taken me a while to realize that part of the reason he'd dated me in the first place was because I was unusually large for an omega. He had assumed, because of that, that I wouldn't like feminine things. Because he was a stereotyping asshole.

Then he'd had the audacity to blame me for his inability to knot me because I wasn't "omega enough."

Being an omega didn't make me less of a man.

Liking pink didn't make me less of a man.

Being taller and broader than average didn't make me less of an omega.

However, I was afraid that tolerating Rex's bullshit for as long as I had did make me less, both as a man and an omega.

It wasn't too late to reclaim some of what I lost though, right?

Milo appeared in the reflection behind me, standing in the doorway. "You look great."

I turned toward him and scanned him up and down. "You look adorable too."

He was wearing jeans, like me, but he had paired them with a patterned baby-blue shirt that made his eyes look more vivid. Even his massive baby belly didn't detract from his appeal.

"You think so?" he asked, tugging on the bottom of his shirt. "I worry that I just look like a bowling ball. How can Everett possibly find me attractive like this?"

My heart went out to him. I crossed the room and pulled him into a hug, pretending his stomach wasn't in the way. After all, it was my little niece or nephew in there and they could never be considered a nuisance.

"Everett will always think you're beautiful." I kissed his cheek. "Consider it part of the mating magic. Even on your grossest day, in your oldest sweatpants, he will still want you."

"Thank you." He sniffed, choked up. "I needed that reminder. My hormones are going haywire. I have swollen feet, and you don't even want to know how many honey-drop sweets I've eaten today. This baby is definitely a bear shifter."

I laughed. "I'm sorry about your feet. Shall we go to the kitchen and check on Momma? She might have something that will help."

He nodded, and we made our way to the kitchen, where Momma was directing a couple of other women, overseeing the production of the New Year's feast with the efficiency of a military commander.

I quietly explained Milo's predicament to her, and she tutted and fetched a herbal tincture for him from the pantry. She showed him how to use it and then insisted he sit and take over her position as supervisor while she and I did some of the busywork.

I appreciated her easy handling of the situation. Milo obviously needed to rest, but he also had to feel like he was contributing because he was still insecure about his place in the family. Her solution accomplished both of those things.

Clever woman.

For the next half hour, we finished preparing the food, and then ferried it outside. The New Year's feast was an informal event but most of the clan usually showed up. Many had helped set up tonight and there was a small fireworks display ready to blast off at midnight.

Clan members gathered around a bonfire in the backyard and I noticed a couple of Dad's enforcers keeping watch to make sure the fire didn't get out of control. Garrick was seated at the bonfire, showing the children how to make s'mores.

I looked around, searching for Knox. He was standing beside one of the food tables, chatting with Jamie, a fox omega with bright red hair and a cute smile. My fists clenched at my sides, and my eyes narrowed. Was that fox flirting with my mate?

I sniffed, although there was no way I'd be able to smell his desire—or lack thereof—from this great of a distance, especially not with so many people around. Still, I couldn't resist the urge to try.

*Ours.*

I sighed. Yes, he was, and he hadn't given me any reason

to think that he was interested in anyone else. We were fated. I had no reason to be jealous. My bear was just insecure because our bond wasn't complete and he was feeling a little possessive.

Knox had been incredibly patient with me. I had no reason not to trust him. As I was thinking that, I made my way to him and tucked myself under his arm. He buried his face in the crook of my neck and breathed me in, scenting me. My bear relaxed.

Our mate was with us and all was right with the world.

I smiled at Jamie. "Hey, how are you doing? How's your mother?"

His mother had dementia and had gradually been slipping downhill over the past few years. He was still caring for her but I didn't think it would be long before she had to go into some kind of special shifter aging facility.

We didn't have one in Grizzly Ridge, and the closest one was an hour's drive away, on the edge of Grayton. Considering the distance, I could understand his reluctance to send her there.

"She's not great." He forced a cheerful expression. "Still relatively fit, but somehow that just seems to make it worse. Her body still thinks she's young, but her mind... Well, you know."

"I'm sorry." I wished there was something I could do to help but diseases like dementia didn't discriminate between shifters and non-shifters. There was no magical cure. If a warlock ever invented one, they'd make a killing.

"It is what it is." He wrung his hands, glancing around as if searching for a distraction. "How is Milo's pregnancy?"

Recalling my earlier conversation with Milo, I grimaced, but I schooled my features quickly. "He's fine. Did you know Knox was out on a job today?"

We chatted for a short while, and then I looped my arm

with Knox's and started my traditional circuit of the main families from Grizzly Ridge.

I liked to use events such as this one as an opportunity to check in with everyone and see how they were going and whether there was anything the Clan Alpha or his family could do to make life easier for them. Often there was nothing, but knowing that we cared went a long way to maintaining healthy clan relationships.

A few minutes before midnight, Dad called us all together for his annual "let's ring in the New Year as a great big happy paranormal family" speech. He talked about all of the good things that happened this last year, highlighted new clan members and babies we'd welcomed, expressed sorrow for the people we lost, and gave a rousing toast to making the most of the New Year.

I poured myself a glass of champagne and grabbed a beer for Knox. Together, we waited for the countdown to midnight. When we reached ten seconds, everyone present began to count out loud.

Nerves crowded my gut, but I was determined to start the New Year off by being brave. As the clan shouted numbers, I drew closer to Knox. My heart raced. Two seconds to go.

Then one.

Fireworks illuminated the sky, bathing the world in starbursts of pink, yellow, and green. I threw my arms around Knox's neck and planted my mouth on his.

He gasped and held me close, his tongue darting out to taste me. I pressed against him, loving the feel of his strong, hard body. My cock twitched and I reluctantly pulled away. I didn't mind public displays of affection but letting my clan smell my arousal was another matter entirely.

Knox stared at me, stunned silent. I grinned mischievously, feeling more like my old self than I had in months. I used to be fun. I used to laugh and tease and play. Maybe I hadn't lost that side of myself.

Maybe I'd just disconnected from him for a while and now we were getting to know each other again. Old friends reunited.

I yanked my shirt off, undid my fly, and peeled down my jeans, only realizing at the last moment that I'd forgotten to take off my shoes. I kicked them off and stumbled as I removed the last of my clothes.

Opposite me, Knox shrugged off his jacket and began to undress as well. My gaze automatically traced the contours of his muscles, but I forced myself to look away.

No getting an erection in front of your family.

I backed away from Knox. "You want another kiss?"

He nodded, his eyes darkening as they locked on my lips.

I blew him one. "Then you'll have to catch me."

With that, I shifted and ran into the woods, hearing his laugh behind me.

# TWENTY-SIX

D*ANNY*

Three days later, as I was wandering back to the bakery after having lunch with Knox, my mind was a fuzzy haze of pleasure and plotting.

How could I get him into bed with me?

I wanted orgasms. Shared orgasms. All we'd done so far was make out—which I loved, no doubt about it—but I was ready for more.

Yes, I was grateful to him for taking it slow and not rushing me. He'd made me feel special and cherished. Like something precious that he wanted to protect.

All of that was good. Honestly. But I was desperate to come with someone other than myself touching me. How should I make that clear to him? Should I present myself to him naked on his bed? Should I simply strip and sit on his cock?

I sighed. Most likely, I ought to talk to the man, which wasn't nearly as fun. But it would have the benefit of avoiding any misunderstanding as well as, you know, dubious consent.

"Danny!"

I stopped walking instantly, almost tripping over my own feet in my fright. I recognized that voice, although I wished I didn't. It was Rex, the man who'd beaten me to a pulp and left me fucking terrified.

My heart beat a staccato rhythm, and I turned toward the voice. Sure enough, there he was. He held my gaze and strode toward me.

My head swam. I'd forgotten to breathe.

I lurched away from him, sprinting as fast as I could, but this time, there was no outrunning him. He grabbed my arm and the scent of burnt coffee filled my nostrils.

"We need to talk," he growled.

"All I need is for you to leave me alone." I tugged my arm, but I wasn't strong enough to pull away from him. "Let me go."

He held firm, and his upper lip curled back in a sneer. "Don't be such a baby."

He dragged me into a narrow alley between the nearest buildings. I planted my feet and tried to resist, but as always, I was weak and he was strong.

"Let me go or I'll scream." I tried to keep my terror under control. "You'll be surrounded before you can get away."

After all, we weren't that far from the center of town and all three of my brothers worked nearby. My mate, too.

"Shut the fuck up." Rex gnashed his teeth at me. "You can scream all you like once you've listened to me. This has gone on for long enough. Call off your family. It's time to stop punishing me and tell the Clan Alpha to let me back into town."

I snorted, hardly able to believe what I was hearing. "Are you kidding me? My dad is never going to welcome you back into Grizzly Ridge. It doesn't matter what I do or say. He knows what you did to me, and if I speak up for you, he'll know that you threatened me. He's not stupid."

Rex released my arm but before I had time to escape, he grabbed onto my wrist, his hand closing around it so tightly that I worried he might break the delicate bones there. It was only by power of will and the determination not to let him see how badly he was hurting me that stopped me from flinching.

"This is all your fault." His eyes flashed yellow-gold, his bear close to the surface. "I have been fucking ostracized because of your weakness. If you were stronger, none of this would have happened. No one would have made a fuss. But because you're weak, they all rushed to condemn me."

My stomach bottomed out. I took a step back, my foot skidding on a piece of gravel. The thing was... he had a point.

Not that I thought it was all right to abuse your partner, but if he'd attacked Everett, Garrick, or Zander, they'd have fought back. They wouldn't have allowed themselves to be hurt the way I had. Or, if for some reason they had, they'd have left him after the first time it happened, not gone back for more.

I wasn't blameless in this.

"Fix it," Rex growled, his eyes glowing brighter.

"Let me go." My voice was quiet, and shame bubbled in my gut.

Why wasn't I yelling at him?

Why hadn't I screamed, as I'd threatened to?

"I can't do what you want me to, and if you hurt me again, you'll only make things worse for yourself. Please, Rex. Just let me go and we can forget about this."

He hesitated, and for a couple of seconds, his grip on my wrist loosened. Sensing that I was making headway, I kept talking.

"You can go back to your cabin, and I'll shower before I see Knox so he doesn't smell you on me. We can—"

His fingers tightened around my wrist and his lips curled into a snarl.

Oh no. I must have said something to piss him off. I racked my mind.

"I heard about that disgusting dog you've been playing with." He backed me up against the side of the building, his breath hot on my face. "You don't belong to him. No matter what happens, you're mine. It's my touch that you'll remember for the rest of your life."

A sliver of ice sliced through me. I was afraid he might be right. I'd already held myself back because of the fear he'd instilled in me. What if I went to my grave still allowing the effects of his violence to dictate my actions?

"I..." I trailed off, trying to make myself as small as possible. It was times like this that I wished I was built like a more traditional omega. It would make it easier to seem meek and nonthreatening. Perhaps that would make his instincts kick in and prevent him from doing anything further to me.

A growl echoed down the alley, sending shivers cascading over my skin.

It hadn't come from Rex.

Slowly, I turned my head. There, at the end of the alley, stood the broad figure of my mate.

# TWENTY-SEVEN

K*NOX*

I was going to kill him.

As I advanced on Danny and the man I assumed was his ex, Rex, I was absolutely certain that no one would miss him if he simply disappeared. All I had to do was tear out his throat and bury the body deep in the woods.

I breathed in, attempting to calm myself, but the sour tang of Danny's fear only aggravated my wolf. The scent was so overpowering that I'd smelled it as I returned to work, and I'd been able to follow the trail right to him.

I felt Danny's gaze on me, but I didn't shift my focus. I couldn't afford to take my eyes off Rex in order to reassure him.

"Get your hands off my mate," I snarled, sizing Rex up as I drew closer.

This was the man who'd abused Danny's trust and made him so wary of others, hesitant to believe in our bond. He was a large guy, as bear shifters often were, with brown hair, a wide chest, thick arms, and a bit too much softness around his belly. His bear stared through his eyes, just as my wolf did mine.

He sneered. "Stop right there, you mangy wolf, or I'll gut him."

I stopped, not because he intimidated me, but because I didn't want to give Danny another reason to be afraid.

There was no way Rex was coming out of this on top. He had perhaps fifty pounds and a couple of inches of height on me, but I had so much more to fight for than he did, and a whole hell of a lot more military training.

"You have one chance to let him go," I said coolly. "I'll count to three, and if you're still here, then I'll be the one gutting you. Three."

Rex didn't seem to even consider taking me up on the offer. He hauled Danny in front of himself and turned toward me, using my mate as a human shield.

"Two." My fingers morphed into claws as I took in the utter lack of color in Danny's cheeks and the way he was sucking in shallow breaths, too scared to move. "One."

Rex dodged as Danny tried to kick his knee. "Come and get me."

I met Danny's gaze and held it until I knew he was seeing me rather than whatever monsters were inside his own mind.

"I won't hurt you," I promised him. "Do you believe me?"

His lips parted, and his tongue flashed out to moisten them. "Yes."

My wolf roared inside me, proud of the trust our mate was putting in us. It was time to let him out.

I shifted, shredding my clothes with my claws, and leaped at Rex, aiming for his head. At the same moment, Danny yanked Rex's forearm from his throat and dropped to the ground. I landed on Rex, knocking him down, pleased when the air hissed from his mouth and he struggled to draw in more.

I fastened my jaws on his throat, tempted to end this right now. All it would take is one bite and Danny would never have to worry about him again. This entire ordeal would be behind us.

"Knox, don't."

I glanced back, caught off guard, and Rex took advantage of my distraction to throw me off him and shift. I readied myself for a fight, but instead, he fled out of the alley.

I took off after him, nipping at his heels, torn between bringing him down quickly and dragging it out to make him suffer. He lashed out, his clawed foot striking my muzzle. I stumbled, but recovered before tripping. Unfortunately, he used the delay to put more distance between us.

I started to speed up but a whimper from somewhere behind me stopped me in my tracks.

*Danny.*

I watched Rex retreat, wanting more than anything to end the threat to my mate, but as Danny whimpered again, I realized that right now he needed my presence more than he needed me to play the part of his personal warrior.

Reluctantly, I turned and trotted back to him. My little bear was crumpled on the ground, his head low, hugging his knees to his chest. I sat beside him, shifted back, and pulled him into my arms, smelling the salt of his tears.

"It's okay," I murmured, kissing the top of his head. "You're all right, baby. I'm here for you."

He fell apart, sobbing on my shoulder. I wrapped one of my arms under his thighs and the other around his back and stood, cradling him against my chest. His eyes widened and he sniffed, his cheeks tear-stained and lips quivering.

"I'm taking you home." I slid my feet into my boots—one of the few items of clothing that had survived my earlier shift—and carried him toward the alley entrance.

He shook his head. "I have to go to work. I'm scheduled for this afternoon, remember?"

A growl rumbled in my chest. "You aren't working like this. They'll make do without you."

"But—"

"No buts. I'm taking care of you, and that's all there is to it." I'd call Garrick and let him know I wouldn't be back as soon as I had Danny tucked up in bed. He wouldn't begrudge me the time to comfort his brother, and I was sure Danny's boss wouldn't mind either.

To my relief, Danny settled into my embrace without further argument. I carried him all the way to his place, ignoring the curious glances of his friends and neighbors. Shifters might be accustomed to nudity, but it was still strange for a man to walk through town naked apart from his shoes in the middle of winter.

When we reached Danny's house, I put him down so he could unlock the door. I then relocked it behind us and guided him to the bathroom. I started the shower and hugged Danny while we waited for the water to warm. Once it was hot enough, I reached for the hem of his shirt, but hesitated.

"Can I undress you?" I asked.

"Yes, please."

He stood passively while I stripped off his clothes, baring his gorgeous body inch by inch. He stepped beneath the spray of water and I kicked off my shoes and followed him in. The fact he didn't speak at all made me nervous. He was usually quite chatty. Rex must have really upset him.

"You aren't... hurt, are you?" I asked, my instincts

screaming for me to check every part of him until I was satisfied there wasn't a single mark on him.

"My wrist hurt earlier, but it's okay now."

I saw red. Gods, I should have torn Rex's throat out. The bastard would have deserved it.

My hands shaking, I grabbed the bar of soap and ran it over Danny's shoulders and chest, down his torso and legs, then up his back, cleaning him thoroughly until my wolf was satisfied that our mate was well.

I washed myself quickly, rinsed off, and shut down the water. I reached across for a towel and passed it to Danny, then took another to dry myself.

"Wait here." I hurried into his bedroom, searched his drawers until I found a pair of cozy flannel pajamas, and took them back to him. "Put these on."

Danny's gaze softened. "Thank you."

He unfolded the pants and pulled them on, then I helped him slide his arms into the shirt and button the front. My heart swelled. Even his puffy red eyes didn't diminish the sweet sight of him in those pajamas.

"You want to take a nap?" I asked.

He hesitated, dozens of emotions crossing his face, but after a moment, he nodded.

"Good." I circled my arm around his waist and walked with him to the bedroom, turning my face to breathe in his scent, no longer soured by fear. I pulled back his blankets and waited for him to get in.

He rested his head on the pillow and watched me, his expression slumberous. "Will you hold me?"

"Sure, baby. I'll just be a minute."

He pouted, but I left him there and headed to the living area, where I used his phone to call Garrick, then the bakery, and lastly, Aaron, to apprise them of the situation.

As expected, Danny's boss was sympathetic and both Garrick and Aaron were furious.

That done, I crawled into bed with my gorgeous mate and spooned him until he fell asleep. I dozed too, caught between sleep and wakefulness, until the doorbell yanked me firmly back to reality.

# CHAPTER
# TWENTY-EIGHT

*D**ANNY**

The murmur of voices woke me. I frowned, my eyes closed, as I realized I could hear at least four different people, and that Knox was no longer pressed reassuringly against me.

I bolted upright, my eyes flying open, and immediately flinched. My family was crowded around the bed, and now that I was more fully conscious, the scent of their anxiety and concern was overwhelming.

I looked around, blinking at Milo, Everett, Garrick, Zander, Dad, and Momma as I tried to make sense of the situation. "What are you all doing here?"

A weight settled onto the bed beside me. Knox. I leaned toward him, drawing comfort from his presence.

"We're here to check on you," Milo said, hovering a little too close.

My pulse pounded in my ears. "Uh... okay. I, um."

Knox kissed my cheek. "Why don't you all wait in the living area? I'll make some coffee and Danny can join us when he's ready."

Dad stiffened for a moment, no doubt bristling at the implied order, but then he straightened and said briskly, "Knox is right. Let's give Danny some space."

They filed out, and as they did so, the tension faded from the room.

I slumped against the pillow. "Thank you."

"No problem." He took my hand. "I'm sorry for letting them in in the first place."

"Don't be." I swallowed to moisten my dry throat. "They wouldn't have taken no for an answer."

He didn't look convinced. "Want me to send them away?"

"No." Not only would that damage the relationship he was slowly building with them, but I did want to see my family. Just not all at once and crowded inside my most private space. "But maybe they can just have a short visit."

Guilt churned in my gut. I should be grateful they'd all rushed here to see me, not be trying to push them away.

"Hey." Knox tapped the end of my nose. "Don't feel bad, okay? Looking after yourself is more important than putting on a show for them."

The guilt dissipated. I'd needed to hear that. "Thanks."

He shook his head, silently dismissing my gratitude. "There's a glass of water on the nightstand. I'll go make the coffee. Come out when you're ready, but don't rush yourself."

He kissed my forehead and sauntered out of the room. It was only then that I realized he was wearing one of my robes. I rolled my eyes at myself. Of course. He'd ruined the outfit he'd been wearing when he'd shifted earlier, and he wasn't keeping any clothes at my place yet. Hopefully, one day soon, he would.

I propped myself up on my elbow and reached for the

glass of water, then drained it in a few mouthfuls. The water soothed my parched throat and I considered just rolling over and going back to sleep. But that would be cowardly. Exactly what Rex had claimed I was. I could do better.

I tugged at the bottom of my pajama shirt, which had ridden up my waist. Should I change into something else?

No. I was comfortable in these, and I didn't want to leave my family waiting for too long. With a sigh, I slung my legs off the edge of the bed, planted my feet on the floor, and stood. I stretched my arms above my head, swiveled the wrist that Rex had hurt earlier to check that everything was in working order, and wandered out.

As I entered the open-plan living area, Knox appeared in front of me with a mug of hot chocolate topped with whipped cream and mini marshmallows.

"Here." He offered it to me.

"Thank you." I took it from him and sipped, keeping my eyes on his. They darkened, perhaps with desire, although I couldn't be sure. "We're making a habit of this."

He smirked. "I'll feed you as many sugar-laden hot chocolates as you want, if it makes you happy."

"Hopefully under better circumstances next time." I was growing tired of him having to rescue me.

Dad joined us. He rested his hand on my shoulder, his fingers brushing the side of my neck. Bears weren't as big on scenting as wolves, but the gesture still reassured me.

"How are you?" he asked, no judgment in his tone.

I inhaled deeply, considering the question before I replied. "I've been better, but I'm all right. You don't have to worry."

His eyes narrowed. "I'll worry about what I like, thank you very much." He gave my shoulder a quick squeeze. "I'm glad to hear it though. Knox took care of you?"

A lump formed in my throat. "Yeah. He, um… So, Rex had cornered me in the alley beside the tattoo parlor, and Knox got me away from him and kept me safe."

He'd brought me home, washed me so tenderly I'd almost burst into tears, and snuggled me until I'd fallen asleep. A boy could get used to that kind of treatment.

I turned to Knox. "Thank you. It was really nice to know I could just let go and count on you."

"You're welcome," he rumbled, his eyes warm with affection.

I bit my lip, looking from one of them to the other. I wanted to know what had happened with Rex—whether anyone had caught him—but I couldn't bring myself to ask. Luckily, Dad seemed to read my mind.

"Everett paid a visit to Rex's cabin, but he wasn't there," he said.

Behind him, Everett growled. "It looked like the asshole had packed a bag and left in a hurry."

At least that was something. If he was on the run, he probably wouldn't bother about harassing me again. Especially not once it became clear that he'd never be welcome in Grizzly Ridge.

"I left him a voicemail."

I looked over at Zander, who was leaning against the wall, his hat in his right hand, his left resting on his hip.

"Everett wanted to do it, but we all know how his temper can be." Zander's lips twitched. "I just reminded him of his agreement with the Clan Alpha and the police and pointed out that if he came within a hundred feet of you again, we'd have every reason to make sure he regretted it."

Everett snorted. "I still think we should have kicked his ass."

Based on the noise Knox made, he agreed. I peeked

around him and Dad, so I could see the rest of the family properly. Everett was sprawled on the couch with Milo on his lap and Momma on the other end. Garrick was perched beside Momma.

My insides warmed. They'd all come here to support me. My mate and family were willing to fight on my behalf. Part of me liked that, but a deeper part of me couldn't help but wish that I was strong enough not to need alphas to defend me.

I wanted to be able to defend myself.

"Come over here, darling." Momma patted the sliver of cushion between herself and Everett. "Squish in and give me some cuddles."

I gladly did as she said, enjoying the sensation of being surrounded by people I loved. Milo detached himself from Everett and snuggled against me. I licked a blob of cream from the top of my hot chocolate.

"Everett, can I have a hot chocolate too?" Milo asked, eyeing it enviously.

"I'll get you one." I heard Everett go to the kitchen.

Momma leaned close. "It's good to see you and Knox getting along."

"It feels good," I admitted. "Right."

"I'm happy for you."

"What did you bake for the kids today?" I asked, needing a distraction from discussing my feelings.

She and Milo told me about the cookies and soup they'd prepared, and then we chatted about a Netflix show that Milo and I both watched religiously.

After a while, Dad made noises about leaving, and I realized that Knox had spoken to him and they were determined to usher everyone to the door.

"Thank you," I whispered to Knox as they departed. "It was nice to see everyone, but I'm ready for it to just be us."

He cocked an eyebrow. "Yeah?"

I nodded, and gestured for him to sit. When he did, I climbed onto his lap. "Knox, can we talk? There's something I should tell you."

# TWENTY-NINE

K NOX

"Yes." There was no way I'd deny him, although I wasn't sure I liked where this was going. I wrapped my arms around Danny and held him close, my wolf rumbling with satisfaction even as my senses were alert for the slightest hint that the situation was about to go downhill.

Danny sighed. "After everything that's happened, I feel like I owe you the truth about what happened between me and Rex."

I frowned. "You don't owe me anything."

He grimaced. "I phrased that wrong. I... I want to tell you. It's just hard for me. Can you be patient?"

"Of course." As if that wasn't all I'd done every day since I'd first smelled him. "You can share as much or as little as you want. There's no pressure."

Danny snuggled against my chest, resting his cheek over my heart. "I know. You've been so patient with me. More than I deserve."

"Not true." I didn't like it when he spoke badly about himself.

"Agree to disagree." He closed his eyes, and I stroked his hair, reveling in its softness. I wondered whether his bear would be this soft to touch. "So, I started dating Rex about a year ago. Maybe a little more. I knew we weren't fated mates, but I figured the chance of meeting my mate in a tiny place like this was slim, so I was open to dating."

A low growl vibrated in my chest, but I cut it off. This was about Danny. Not me.

"Rex always had a bit of a chip on his shoulder about traditional gender roles and stereotypes. He liked that I was bigger than most omegas because he thought it meant that I was stronger and could handle more than them. In hindsight, perhaps he believed it meant he could hurt me more before I broke. But he still wanted me to behave in the way he thought an omega should. Subservient. If I acted too much like an alpha, he saw it as a threat to his masculinity."

"Asshole," I muttered.

He tipped his head in acknowledgment. "Yet he didn't like me showing my softer side either. He said it made me weak. I could never tell what he wanted from me. There was no winning."

My poor baby. I could imagine how confusing that must have been.

"It took me a while to see through him. I was blind to the red flags. He was impossible to please, and jealous too. At first, his jealousy made me feel special. Until it didn't."

My stomach soured. I knew I'd be possessive of him if he ever allowed me to claim him. My beast considered him ours. I couldn't help it. But I'd have to try to rein it in so I didn't remind him of his ex.

That was, assuming he gave me a chance. I hoped the fact he was willing to talk about this and had called me his mate meant he was—or at least, that he would be—in the future.

"He'd always make little comments if I didn't behave in a way he thought was appropriate for an omega, or if he believed I was flirting with someone else—not that I ever was. At first I didn't think much of it, but that must have encouraged him because he got bolder and began to make me a bit uncomfortable."

It was only by force of will that I managed to keep my claws sheathed. Somehow, I knew this story was about to take a turn.

"He got meaner. I guess it was a type of emotional abuse. He'd belittle me and I just took it because I was honestly so shocked. I didn't know how I'd been so wrong about him, or what to do about it. I tried to leave him once, but he convinced me he'd just been awful because of something bad that had happened at work, so I stayed."

"Breathe, baby," I urged as his scent adopted a bitter undertone. "You don't have to be scared. I've got you."

He drew in a deep breath and let it out in a gust. "Thank you." He nuzzled my chest. "Um, so one day, I was home late from work and he thought I'd been with another alpha. He, uh, he hit me."

I stiffened, my vision sharpening as my eyes changed. I closed them, not wanting to give him any reason to fear me.

"Did it happen more than once?" I asked, my voice modified by the fangs that had dropped, itching to tear out Rex's throat.

He nodded. "I was so ashamed of myself for allowing it to happen that I didn't feel like I could tell anyone, and he threatened to beat me worse if I left."

"So, how'd it finally end?" What—or who—did I owe my thanks to for saving Danny?

"He attacked me one night. He was sure I'd been cheating on him. I hadn't, but that didn't make any difference. I... I thought he was going to kill me. Everett turned up and caught him. He fought Rex off and told him to leave town."

This time, I couldn't suppress a growl. I should never have let Rex leave that alley alive. I should have ripped his head off his neck and ensured he could never hurt, threaten, or scare my omega ever again.

Danny curled into a ball, making himself smaller in my arms. "I hate that Everett saw me like that, and that he took me home to Momma, so the whole family could see what had happened. Suddenly, everyone in town seemed to know how weak I'd been."

"You weren't weak." My voice was almost inhuman. Rage coursed through my veins, but I managed my reaction as best I could. Losing my shit wouldn't help him. "You were strong, and I'm proud of you for surviving that."

He shook his head. "I didn't fight back."

He was obviously ashamed, and I hated it. He had no reason to be.

"You kept yourself alive. None of what happened is on you. Your trust was broken. That's not your fault. It's his."

Danny sniffled. "I should have left before it got to that point, or seen the warning signs. Gods know they were there."

My gut twisted. "Don't be so hard on yourself, baby. Things are always clearer in hindsight. You made the best choices you could at the time."

He scoffed, but didn't speak.

Tentatively, I kissed the top of his head. The need to comfort him was almost overwhelming, but I was afraid to come on too strong and scare him away.

"What else is going on in here?" I asked, tapping his temple gently.

The dampness of his tears soaked fabric, and my wolf howled internally, horrified that our mate was upset. I breathed through my mouth so as not to smell the salty tang of his misery.

"Rex was right," he sobbed, burying his face in the fabric. "I'm weak."

"No, you're not."

He whimpered. "But I am. None of my brothers would have let their partner bully them or hurt them."

I gritted my teeth and clung to the fraying threads of my temper. "Firstly, you can't know that."

"But—"

"Secondly," I continued without pausing. "Your brothers are alphas. I know we're all equal in the eyes of the law, but physically, they're stronger and they heal faster. You can't hold yourself to the same standard as them when something that would only inconvenience them temporarily could kill you."

I'd rather he was cautious and kept himself alive than behaved recklessly in an effort to be more like his alpha brothers.

Danny tilted his face toward me. The glossy sheen on his rich brown eyes flayed me. If I had my way, he'd never have a reason to cry again.

"Milo was kidnapped, and he fought back," he whispered. "He's only human, and he was pregnant, and he still tried to get away."

I brushed his hair off his face, resisting the urge to trace his features with my fingertips. "The attack on Milo was by a stranger. Rex spent time building a level of trust with you. He tore you down so slowly that you couldn't have been expected to see what was happening."

"I had more time, more support, more... everything. I'm a coward."

I racked my mind for a way to stop him from sounding

so defeated. "Have you ever heard of the way some people boil crabs alive?"

He looked at me as though I was a monster.

"Not me," I added defensively. "The point is, they put a crab in a pot of cold water and slowly heat it until it's too late and the crab is being cooked alive. Your relationship was like that. You can't blame yourself for not realizing that the water around you was gradually heating up."

Danny blinked up at me, his eyelashes clumped and wet. "People really do that?"

"Yeah."

His face twisted with disgust. "That's awful."

He was getting sidetracked. That wasn't the point.

I sighed. Perhaps I owed him a truth of my own. "Thank you for telling me about Rex. There's something I'd like to share with you too."

CHAPTER

# THIRTY

**D***ANNY*

Was this when he would finally reject me?

I pressed myself closer to Knox, my eyes itchy, my nose running, and my heart hammering at a thousand miles an hour. His chest was warm against me, but the steady thump-thump-thump had sped up enough that I worried about what was to come. He was clearly nervous.

I'd confessed the sordid truth. He knew now how pathetic I was. A man like Knox deserved someone strong. Someone tougher than me.

Nevertheless, I'd accept his comfort for as long as I could. I'd revel in his scent and pretend I belonged on his lap, comfortable and safe.

Knox cleared his throat. "You know I grew up in a pack?"

"I assumed as much." Most wolves did, even if they became loners later.

"We were very traditional." He grimaced. "Fucking archaic, actually. My father was the Pack Alpha."

My breath caught, and I tugged my lower lip between

my teeth. If Knox's father had been Pack Alpha, then by rights, he should have inherited the title. Why was he here and not leading his pack?

Knox raised his eyes and looked somewhere above my head. "He was power-hungry, and he saw me as a threat. He'd never have handed over control of the pack willingly, and he was afraid I'd try to take it from him. Even though he believed that shifters should live separately from humans, he had me enlisted in the military to get me off pack lands."

My chest squeezed. I didn't understand. Alphas passed on leadership of their pack or clan to one of their children—unless someone else challenged them for the role and won. It was just how things were.

One day, Garrick would supersede Dad as Clan Alpha, but Dad had never viewed him as a threat. Instead, he'd gladly shown him how to be a good leader and ensure the smooth running of the clan for the future. When the time came, he'd step down and enjoy his golden years without the weight of the clan on his back.

Obviously, Knox's father had viewed the situation differently.

"I returned to the pack when Mom got sick." His fists clenched, and I wondered if he was even aware of it. "I wanted to be with her. Dad wasn't exactly a doting mate, and I was their only child, so she didn't have anyone else."

Oh, Knox. My heart ached for him and his mother. Our clan was always supportive of anyone who was going through a hard time, so I couldn't imagine how alone they must have felt.

"Soon after Mom died, Dad attacked me. I think he was afraid that I wouldn't leave again, and that I might challenge him now that Mom wasn't around to talk me out of it." He swallowed, his Adam's apple bobbing. "He snuck up on me while I was sleeping and tried to rip my heart out."

I flinched, my lips parting with a gasp. My gaze flew to his chest, where the knotted scar lay beneath his shirt. A scar I now knew must be from his father's claws. Although, even if his father had buried his claws in Knox's chest, the wound should have healed without leaving a mark.

Knox saw where my gaze lingered and laughed bitterly. "He'd tipped his claws with silver. Even though I woke up and managed to fight him off, the poison would have killed me if not for one of the pack's warlocks, who caught me fleeing and took pity on me. Her magic saved my life."

I was glad Knox had had her. If not, I might never have met him. I shivered as that thought struck home. I could have lost my mate before I even knew he existed.

"I fled and my father announced that I'd been exiled for attacking him and would be executed if I ever set foot on the pack lands again. Everyone there was forbidden from communicating with me."

"I'm so sorry." He'd been forced to leave his home, probably the only home he'd ever known besides the military, and all because his father was a power-hungry maniac.

He shrugged. "It is what it is. I don't miss the people. Most of them were too easily led, but I miss the land I grew up on, and I worry that I won't ever have that sense of belonging anywhere again. I won't be able to recognize the smell of the soil that identifies the land as being home, or know the wildlife that lives in an area. I won't ever be welcomed or accepted because I'm a wolf without a pack. An outcast."

An exile.

My gut clenched. There wasn't much worse for a wolf than being exiled, although at least Knox had avoided being branded so he could hide his status if he chose.

Yet people would be wary of him anyway. Just as my clan had been.

Guilt tightened in my chest. If I'd been more receptive to Knox when he'd arrived in Grizzly Ridge, then my clan might have accepted him, but instead I'd been too busy fighting my own demons to realize how much I was hurting him.

I'd made him unwelcome. An outsider in a place that should have been his salvation.

I was an asshole.

Tears burned in the backs of my eyes and my throat clogged with emotion.

"I'm sorry." I kissed the underside of his jaw. "I'm so sorry. I hate that that happened, and I hate how I've treated you, and how we've all kept you at a distance. You don't deserve that. I wish I could undo it all."

"Hey, now." He gazed down at me, affection shining in his eyes. "You have nothing to be sorry for. Just being with you and having a job that isn't solitary is the most I've felt like part of a community for years."

Sorrow clawed at my insides. If that was the case, I felt even worse for him. I wanted to hunt down his father and see how he liked having his heart ripped out with poisoned claws and his reputation tainted.

Knox deserved so much better than his lot in life.

"How about we get something to eat and watch a movie?" he suggested. "I'll cook, since you've been through the emotional wringer. What do you say?"

"Yes, please," I whispered, feeling lazy and ungrateful and cherished and protected all at the same time.

"Do you like burgers?" he asked, lifting my weight off his lap and setting me on the cushion beside him. I rested my head against the back of the sofa and watched as he stood and ran his hand through his hair.

I snorted. "Do I like burgers? I love them. Do you know a predatory shifter that doesn't?"

He grinned. "Wait here. I'll be back soon."

As he left, my heart warmed. I couldn't help but think that there might actually be a chance we could work all of this out.

So when Knox returned a while later, toting burgers and a steaming cup of lemon and honey, I turned to him and asked, "Do you think you could be happy in Grizzly Ridge?"

# CHAPTER
# THIRTY-ONE

*NOX*

Two days after the evening when Danny and I exchanged secrets and I'd confessed that I wanted nothing more than to forge a future here with him, I pulled my motorcycle up outside my cabin.

I removed my helmet, and glanced up as a fat drop of rain splattered on my forehead. It was cold and about to pour at any second, but that wasn't the reason I froze, instantly on alert. It was the sickly sweet stench of blood and decay that stopped me in my tracks.

I breathed in quietly. The scent that filled my nostrils was at least a day or so old. My wolf rumbled beneath the surface of my skin; his ears pricked for the sound of heartbeats or the rustle of clothes, but there was nothing. Almost complete silence. It was eerie.

Of course, if someone was still here, they'd have heard me roar up on my Harley. They were probably frozen, just as I was, in the hopes I wouldn't notice them. It was more likely that they'd been and gone while I was staying with Danny.

I cocked my head, debating my next steps. My instincts

told me not to approach the front entrance, so I took off my shoes to muffle my footfalls and tiptoed around to the back door. A large, dark lump was splayed on the doorstep.

I retched, my stomach trying to turn itself inside out. Acid burned up the inside of my throat and the awful sour-bitter taste of bile hit my tongue. I spat, but the unpleasantness lingered.

Slowly, reluctantly, I raised my head again.

I approached the huddled form with trepidation. A fly buzzed, and I smacked it away from the dead wolf. Its eyes were glazed, its throat a bloody pulp. Maggots crawled in its flesh, and my stomach rolled again. I swallowed, suppressing the urge to throw up.

Who the hell had done this?

I dropped to my knees beside the wolf. It must have been beautiful once, with lush gray fur and a strong body.

Grief latched its claws into me.

I shifted, shook off my clothes, and then laid myself alongside the wolf.

I howled.

I cried out to alert the whole of Grizzly Ridge that something terrible had been done, but I couldn't bring myself to look at the wolf again.

It wasn't a shifter. Perhaps that would bring some people relief, but in my shifted form, it made the situation worse. This animal hadn't hurt anyone. It had just been living its life when someone had snuffed it out in an attempt to threaten and intimidate me.

What a fucking tragedy.

I howled again, letting loose the full force of my emotions.

Zander arrived first.

I recognized his scent as he rounded the corner and bowled toward me. Instantly I was on my feet, snarling and ready to defend the fallen wolf. To protect its dignity in death.

Zander shifted back, standing a few yards from me.

"Whoa. It's okay, Knox. I don't want to hurt him. I just need to take a look. What happened?"

I crouched over the wolf, reluctant to step aside.

"I'll treat him respectfully," he promised, getting low to avoid towering over me. "Will you change out of your fur and let me know what's going on here?"

I hesitated. Zander didn't mean the fallen wolf any harm. He wanted to help. Logically, I knew that's exactly what I needed, but fighting my instincts proved difficult.

Someone had killed this beautiful creature because of me—I had absolutely no doubt of that—which meant that caring for it was my responsibility.

"I won't even touch him." Zander edged forward. "All right?"

Finally, I shifted. Tears stung my eyes.

"I just got home." My voice sounded distant, as if I were listening to myself through a layer of molasses. "It's the first time I've been here since Wednesday. I found him like that."

Zander's expression softened. "I'm sorry. It looks like he's been here since yesterday, at least. Possibly earlier."

I nodded. "Agreed. This is"—I swallowed my emotions —"intended to be a threat, I think."

Walking closer now that I wasn't growling to keep him at a distance, Zander examined the fatal wound to the wolf's throat.

"Do you think it was Rex?" he asked, reaching toward the wolf but stopping before he touched it, clearly remembering his promise not to lay his hands on it. "This could have been done not long after you chased him out of town."

"It's possible." I sniffed, sifting through the layers of

scent, but then growled, frustrated. "The smell of decay is too strong. I can't tell if Rex's scent is there too, hiding beneath it."

Zander's nostrils flared, and I assumed he was testing whether his own nose could pick up anything useful. "You're right. We'll pay him a visit anyway."

"Damn right, we will." I straightened and balled my fists at my sides. "That asshole has a lot to answer for. If he—"

"Not you." Zander cut me off. "My team. This is a police matter."

"The fuck it is. This is a threat from a coward who's too scared to face me head-on."

"Knox." He laid his hand on my shoulder and I glared at him until he removed it. "I can't condone you dealing with this personally. We don't even know for sure it was Rex. You've made no secret of the fact you're investigating the rogue wolf pack. It could have been them."

I clenched my jaw, mentally preparing a list of the reasons that Rex deserved my fist in his face, but before I got the chance to voice them, I heard flat shoes slapping against the pavement and then Melinda Blackwood rounded the corner.

Her gaze went straight to the wolf and she made a pained sound in the back of her throat. She raised her eyes to me, the gold of her bear shining through. I turned stiff as she threw her arms around me and hugged me tight.

# THIRTY-TWO

**D**ANNY

I was opening the oven to pull out a chocolate croissant a customer had asked us to reheat when Milo burst through the kitchen door, his face cherry-red and his shirt hitched up to reveal a sliver of his swollen belly.

"What's wrong?" I asked, setting the tray with the croissant down on a wooden board.

He bent over, grabbing the counter to steady himself and puffing as he struggled for breath. "Something bad has happened at Knox's place."

My legs went weak and I stumbled, catching myself on the counter.

My mate was in trouble.

I shoved myself upright. I had to go to him. Right now. But the buzz of customers through the door reminded me that I was in the middle of a busy shift.

"Don't panic." Milo had uncurled himself and seemed to be getting his breathing under control. "Sorry, I ran all the way here. Everett said that Knox is okay but he might

177

need some support. He howled so loudly that Zander heard him and called for backup."

"Okay." I sucked in a lungful of air and released it in a whoosh, gathering myself. "Thanks for telling me."

What next?

I couldn't leave—or at least, I shouldn't—but I had to. Knox had been there for me when I needed him time and time again. There was no way I could live with myself if I wasn't present for him when he needed me.

"Danny!" my boss called from behind the serving counter. "We need you out here."

I froze in place, torn between leaving immediately and doing as the boss said.

"Go," Milo urged, waving me away. "I'll stay and help."

Relief flooded me, loosening my muscles and helping me to breathe easier. "Thank you."

He wouldn't be able to do everything I could, but knowing that my boss would have an extra set of hands available reduced my guilt to a level where I didn't feel like a terrible employee.

I stripped off my apron, handed it to Milo, and slunk out the back door. As I hurried around the side of the bakery and onto the main street, I debated whether to go home to get my car or head straight to Knox's. It was hard to know which would be faster.

I decided to go straight there, so I hurried along the sidewalk, pushing to run faster than a human would be able to. I turned several corners, barely paying attention to where I was going as I allowed the slight tug inside my chest to lead me to my mate.

I took comfort from the presence of that connection. Perhaps it was insubstantial because we hadn't properly mated yet, but I knew that I'd be able to sense if Knox had been badly injured. The delicate tether between us would begin to fray.

As I turned the corner onto the road his cabin was on, I spotted a police car parked outside. My chest tightened, and it wasn't only from the exertion. I should never have parted from Knox this morning. I should have insisted he come to work with me and sit at a table, drink coffee, and eat pie all day. I'd happily keep him in supply.

There wasn't anyone stationed in front of his house, so I rushed around the back, coming up short at the sight of two naked men standing with the uniformed deputies Hawk and Clay.

My eyes narrowed. Shifters might be blasé about nudity, but my bear didn't like seeing our mate naked around other men. Even if they were all alphas.

"Knox," I cried, plastering myself against his body—partly because I wanted to be close to him and partly to hide his thick cock and muscular chest from the view of any potential admirers. "Are you okay?"

"Danny." A crease formed between his eyebrows, and he ducked his head and scented me. I relaxed against him. I hadn't realized how terrified I'd been that I might find him injured until I was finally sure he was safe." What are you doing here?"

"That's on me." Everett's voice came from behind Zander. "I told Milo to get him."

My eldest brother stepped aside so I could see Everett, and my blood chilled when I realized what he was crouching over.

A dead wolf.

I unwound one of my arms from around Knox and raised my trembling hand to my mouth. "What is this?"

"That's what I'd like to know." Zander sounded disgruntled.

"It must be a threat, right?"

Zander nodded. "But from whom?"

"Rex." I couldn't imagine who else would hate Knox enough to do this. I scanned each person present. The doubt on both the deputies' faces and Zander's was clear. They thought I was wrong. "You agree with me, right, Ev?"

Everett glanced down at the wolf. "I've seen what Rex is capable of firsthand, and yeah, I think he could have done this."

"Then we need to make him pay." The words emerged from beneath gritted teeth. I was sick of Rex toying with me. I wanted him out of my life so that I never even had to think of him again.

"We don't have any proof." Zander's tone was gentle but firm. "We'll follow all leads, but without evidence, we can't take action."

My mouth opened and closed. "Are you kidding? That's not good enough, Z!"

"Hey." Knox's arms tightened around me. "It's okay."

Tears sprang to my eyes, and I blinked rapidly, trying futilely to hide them. "No, it's not. No one is allowed to threaten my mate and get away with it. Especially not a lowlife like Rex, and especially not because of me."

It wasn't fair. Knox shouldn't have to deal with this kind of brutality because of my bad taste in men. Nor should that poor wolf have had to die. All of this could have been avoided if I'd been smarter or stronger.

Knox took hold of my chin. "I've always been a trouble-maker, but being with you is the best reason I've ever had to cause trouble. This isn't going to scare me off."

I stepped back and straightened my spine, ignoring his hands when they dropped from my hips. "In that case, I'm sticking to you like a bee to honey until we've proven that this was Rex and he's locked away somewhere. You're staying with me."

Knox's lips parted and his eyes widened. He looked almost excited, but then the expression was wiped from his face. "I don't want to encroach on your space or make you uncomfortable."

"You won't." I raised my chin. "I'm not taking no for an answer."

# CHAPTER
# THIRTY-THREE

*Nox*

I raised my fist to knock on Aaron and Melinda's front door with my other hand in Danny's and a bottle of spiced honey whiskey tucked under my arm.

"You don't have anything to worry about." Danny repeated the same thing he'd said several times now, as if that would somehow make me worry less. "You know my family. You've talked to each of them several times. You work with Garrick and Everett. I'm not sure why you're so nervous."

I narrowed my eyes at him. If he didn't look so cute wrapped in a soft knitted sweater with a woolen hat pulled low over his forehead, I might have scowled. As it was, I didn't have the heart. Or rather, my heart melted every time I looked at him and I knew I'd let him get away with whatever he wanted.

"Your parents still haven't said whether they approve of me," I pointed out.

This was relevant. Especially since Aaron was the Clan Alpha. If he disapproved of our relationship, he had the power to make things very difficult for us.

Danny huffed. "Momma loves you, and Dad is grateful to you for helping protect the omegas in his care."

I arched an eyebrow, silently questioning this.

"Me, Milo, and George," he said, checking the names off on his fingers.

I snorted. "Milo wouldn't have needed help if not for me, and anyone could have found George. As for you..." I felt myself soften. "As if I wouldn't protect my mate until my very last breath."

"Aww." He kissed my cheek. "But seriously. Don't stress. It will be fine."

Fine. Yeah, he was filling me with confidence.

"Shouldn't someone have answered the door by now?" I asked.

Danny sniffed, so I did too. The scent of barbecued meat was thick in the air.

"They're probably around the back, using the grill." He tried the handle and it opened. "Come on."

Keeping my hand in his, he led me through the house and out through the sliding glass doors onto the deck. He didn't let go of me as we joined the others, and my chest puffed with pride. He was claiming me, even if it was only subtle. By holding my hand, he was showing his family that we were together, and that he was proud to be with me.

My wolf rumbled with pleasure.

Several people I recognized from around town but whose names I didn't know were gathered on the deck, chatting. It was damn cold outside this evening, the air crisp and the first hints of frost already settling on the grass, but no one seemed to mind.

I sought out Aaron and offered him the spiced honey whiskey.

He accepted the bottle and read the label. "Thanks. This

looks like a good one. You'll have to join me for a glass later."

"Sounds good." I relaxed a little. Perhaps Danny was right and I didn't need to be so concerned about how his parents might view our relationship.

"Come and grab a grilled steak," Garrick called, flipping a hunk of still-red meat off the grill and onto a plate beside it. "Danny, there's seared salmon on the table."

Danny grinned. "Thanks."

I allowed him to lead me to the table, where he helped himself to salmon, and then over to the grill, where Garrick passed me a plate laden with a juicy, rare steak.

"Wolves like steak, right?" he asked.

I chuckled. "Wolves like most meat."

"Good. You'll fit right in."

My heart warmed, and I turned away so he wouldn't see the emotion flickering across my face.

Danny squeezed my hand. "Let's find a seat."

"Sure."

We weaved between members of the Grizzly Ridge clan until Danny found a cluster of chairs near the sliding doors. Milo was slumped on one of them, and Everett hovered over him. Danny sat beside Milo and exchanged a look with him. I wondered what that was about.

"Why did Aaron call this clan meeting?" I asked, claiming the chair on Danny's other side.

Everett's gaze left Milo briefly. "He wanted to get the message out about possible threats in town. He doesn't want anyone caught off guard."

I frowned. "But surely he doesn't want to scare people either."

Everett shrugged. "He and Garrick made the decision. I guess they thought it would be worth it."

Considering this, I chowed down on the steak, keeping

an eye on Danny to make sure he remembered to eat too. My little bear could be distractible.

Once most of the people gathered were enjoying their dinner, Aaron stood and cleared his throat. I wondered if he got sick of hosting these get-togethers. Whenever my dad summoned the clan, they had to go out of their way to please him, not vice versa. I couldn't imagine him trying to feed everyone or make the occasion enjoyable like Aaron and Melinda did.

"Thank you all for coming. I know this was a bit out of the blue, but we've been experiencing some unfortunate issues in Grizzly Ridge recently and I wanted to let you know to be on your guard." He continued, telling the assembled clan members to alert him, Zander, or one of the enforcers if they spotted any unknown shifters—particularly wolves—in town, or if they saw or smelled Rex.

He went on to explain what had happened with the wolf left at my door. There were a few grumblings at that. No shifter liked wildlife to be harmed. Well, unless it was something they'd hunted and eaten. Wasteful death bothered us far more than it did most humans.

When Aaron finished, I was surprised when he turned toward us and announced that Danny had a few words to say.

"Danny?" I murmured questioningly.

Danny rose to his feet and put his hands behind his back, as if hoping no one would be able to sense his nerves if they couldn't see him shaking. What was he doing?

"If I find out that any of you are connected to this—that you're assisting Rex or are trying to chase Knox away—then I'll make sure you're held accountable." He spoke with more surety than I'd have expected. "I know it took me a while to warm up to Knox, but I've never wanted him gone and I won't tolerate anyone else being unwelcoming toward him. He's here to stay."

My insides turned to mush. I stared up at Danny, hardly able to believe my ears.

He'd defended me. To his entire clan.

He sat and took my hand. Whispers rippled through the crowd, and to my astonishment, I heard people agreeing with him. George. Craig the butcher. Grumpy Ray. Yuri and Li.

My heart threatened to burst.

I nuzzled Danny, brushing my lips over the sensitive skin behind his ear. "Thank you."

He shivered, the musky sweetness of his arousal curling around me. "You can thank me properly later."

# THIRTY-FOUR

D*ANNY*

I was practically vibrating with need as we made our way up the path to my front door. Knox's arm was around me, and he smelled of leather, pine, and lust.

I wanted him.

It was as if... once I'd stopped denying my attraction to Knox and my determination to make our mating work, all of the desire for him that I'd been suppressing had broken free, washing over me like a tsunami, threatening to pull me under.

I was tempted to let it.

Summoning the last of my patience, I withdrew my key from my pocket and hurried up the stairs. I slotted it into the door and turned. The door creaked open.

I shoved it, impatient to get Knox naked, then I backed him against the wall and dropped to my knees in front of him.

He gazed down at me, his eyes nearly black in the dim light. "Are you sure—"

I yanked his zipper down, cutting him off. "I know

exactly what I want. Unless you have any protests, please don't finish that question."

He held his hands up, placating. "No protests here."

"Excellent." I grabbed the sides of his jeans and tugged them down to reveal his briefs. Those dropped too, and now both pieces of clothing were hanging around his knees.

Without another word, I swallowed him.

He shouted and bucked, lodging himself deeper in my throat. I choked, and he drew back, apologies spilling from his lips, but I grabbed his left hip and refused to let him retreat any further. With my right hand, I gripped his cock and then I pressed my lips to the tip.

First I sucked the head of his cock into my mouth. Thick, red, and desperate. Salty with precum. Then I stretched my lips, taking him further, until he bumped against the back of my throat. He groaned and threaded his fingers through my hair. I looked up at him, my eyes watering, and silently urged him to take control.

A muscle ticked in his jaw. His nostrils flared but he handled me as if I were made of the most precious china.

"If it's too much, tap my hip," he ordered.

"Mm-hmm," I hummed around his cock.

"Fuck." He gave a shallow thrust into my mouth and began to rock back and forth, feeding me a little more each time.

I moaned to show my appreciation. I didn't want him to think I didn't love this. Every second that his heavy alpha cock rested on my tongue was bliss. I hollowed out my cheeks and closed my eyes, focusing on the slide of his silken skin and the delicious taste of his desire.

"Look at me," he snarled.

My cock strained, made eager by the roughness of his voice.

That roughness was because of me. He was desperate for me.

The musky scent of slick filled the air. I opened my eyes, blinking when my eyelashes stuck together. Saliva dribbled down my chin. I must have looked wrecked, but he just swiped the pad of his thumb beneath my eye, gathering the moisture there, and licked it up.

His cock thickened in my mouth, and I dug my fingers into his ass cheek, desperate for more.

"I'm on the edge," Knox warned. "I've wanted you for too long. Unless you want me to come in your mouth, you need to stop now."

I pulled off, but not for the reason he thought. "I want you inside me."

He stared at me, stunned. "Are you s—" He cut himself off just in time to avoid my wrath. "How do you want me?"

I cocked my head, surprised in turn. In my experience, alphas simply put you where they wanted you and went to town. "Can I ride you?"

"Fuck yes." He kicked off his shoes and shucked his jeans and underwear, then offered me his hand. When I placed mine in it, he pulled me to my feet. "Bedroom or sofa?"

I considered the options for a moment. "Sofa."

It would be easier to get leverage there.

He swept me into his arms and carried me over.

I giggled, clinging to him. "I'm heavy!"

"Not to me."

He set me gently on the sofa and sat on the cushion beside me, pulling his shirt off over his head and leaving himself bare. My greedy eyes drank up the view. His strong chest was tattooed, as was his shoulder and one upper arm. The intricate ink curved around his musculature, forming knots and patterns.

His cock, flushed and red, stood proudly from a small thatch of dark hair, and his thighs walked a fine line between being lean and deliciously thick.

Goldilocks thighs. Just right for this little bear.

I pulled off my knitted sweater and reached for the hem of my shirt, but he covered my hand with his, stopping me.

"Let me." His tongue flicked out to wet his lips. "I want to savor this."

"O-Okay."

I stood, not quite sure what to do with my arms. He knelt in front of me and lifted the hem of my shirt. He inched it up, his lips following the fabric, dropping kisses right above the waistband of my jeans, then along my treasure trail to my belly button, where he paused to nuzzle me.

My breath hitched. No one had ever taken their time with me like this.

He rose and peeled the shirt over my head, then tossed it aside. I expected him to move on to my jeans, but instead he flicked my nipple with his thumb and bent to suck on it. I groaned as heat shot from my nipple to my groin. I'd always loved having them played with.

Slick soaked my underwear. Knox's gaze met mine and a smug smile curled his lips. I'd have been tempted to wipe it off if he didn't look as desperate as I was, with flushed cheeks and eyes that were nearly black, flashing with green each time his wolf looked out through them.

He removed my jeans and underwear with the same level of care, trailing kisses down the inside of my thigh, pausing when he reached my knee. A shiver rippled through me and I didn't resist as he urged me to recline on the sofa. He licked a stripe from the inside of my knee to my ankle, then undid my shoelaces and took off my shoes, jeans, and underwear.

I lay before him, naked and horny, my upper thighs streaked with slick.

His wolf eyed me hungrily. I wouldn't mind him devouring me.

He dropped to his knees and licked up the slick that decorated my thighs, his chest rumbling with pleasure. He looked at my cock like he was about to eat it, but I pushed him away.

"If you put your mouth on me, I'll come," I said.

He didn't look like he understood the problem.

"I want you inside me," I reminded him.

His eyes flickered brown, then green, and his chest heaved as he tore himself away from me and mimicked my position on the sofa.

"Ride the cum out of me, baby."

My ass throbbed, more than ready for his big alpha cock. I straddled him and positioned my hole against the head of his cock.

Slowly, I lowered myself down.

He stretched me, but I relished the slight burn. He grabbed my hips, his fingernails digging into the tender flesh there, providing a sting to accompany the pleasure of his thick shaft entering me.

Evidence of how badly he wanted me.

He shuddered as he bottomed out inside me, his hair rasping deliciously against my sensitive ass. I rose up and lowered myself again, throwing my head back and closing my eyes as his cock bumped against my prostate.

I whimpered. "Gods, you feel good."

"You're so tight, Danny." He growled the words, which were almost incomprehensible. His hands traveled around to the globes of my ass and flexed. "This is mine now. Got it?"

"Yes." I rode him, forcing my eyes open so I could watch the play of pleasure and emotion across his face.

"Mine," he snarled. "No one else gets to touch you."

"No one." It was all I could do to agree. My cock bounced, slapping my abdomen each time I came down firmly against Knox.

"I'll end them if they do."

I shouldn't like the sound of that, but I did. It promised protection and possession and belonging. Precum leaked from my tip, smearing my abs.

"Understand?" he demanded, bucking his hips to slam up into me.

"Yes," I babbled helplessly. "I want that. I want you. You, and no one else. I'm yours. All yours. I promise."

He bared his teeth, showing his fangs. Slick gushed from me, making an obscene *slap-slap-slap* noise with each thrust.

His eyes were conflicted, changing from brown to green and back again. No doubt his wolf was urging him to claim me with a mating bite and the human part of him was resisting. I appreciated his restraint and felt a pang of guilt for not being ready for that step yet.

But then his cock swelled, pressing against my sweet spot, and I couldn't think of anything else.

I cried out, spurting all over him as I came, pleasure rolling through me in waves.

"Fuck." Knox's grip tightened on my hips. His fingers would no doubt leave marks. He thrust up, seating himself deeply inside me, then filled me, painting my insides with his cum.

His cock continued to swell, locking him inside me, so large I could hardly breathe. I flopped against him, wincing when it tugged at the rim of my hole. His arms looped around me and he nuzzled me, peppering lazy kisses across my face and head.

"I've never been knotted before," I admitted, resting my cheek on his pec. Rex had never been able to knot me, even though he should have, being an alpha. He'd blamed it on me being not "omega" enough, but that was bullshit. If anything he wasn't *alpha* enough. Perhaps that was why he'd tried to prove his strength in other ways.

Knox found my lips with his and kissed me tenderly. "And you never will be by anyone else."

"I won't," I agreed, resting limply against him.

I liked the knot. It joined us together in a way that couldn't be denied, even if we didn't have a bite to connect us yet.

"Thank you for trusting me," he murmured, stroking my hair. "And for what you said at the gathering."

I grimaced. "I should have made my position clear sooner."

"Position." He chuckled and nudged me with his nose.

I rolled my eyes. "I thought you were supposed to be the mature one. How old are you anyway?"

As he reached down and wrapped his hand around my cock, any trace of humor fled. I groaned, shocked when my cock began to plump. I'd never have thought I could rally so quickly. He was still inside me.

Apparently, we were both sex-crazed for each other.

"I'm going to make you come until you forget any 'should haves,'" he whispered beside my ear.

I groaned. "I've created a monster."

And you know what?

I wasn't mad about it.

CHAPTER

# THIRTY-FIVE

K*NOX*

My mind swam with sleep as a hot, wet, sucking heat fastened around my cock. I thrust lazily, caught in an erotic dream in which Danny was sitting on my face. The suction on my cock was out of place. It confused me.

I blinked, my vision blurry as I tried to make sense of what was going on.

I was in a bed, but not my own.

Danny's.

My body was warm and languid, sated from two rounds of lovemaking. The blankets in front of me were tented, and beneath them I could see my mate positioned between my thighs, swallowing my cock like his life depended on it.

Fuck. My hips arched, chasing pleasure, but he pinned me down. The display of strength turned me on. I was easily stronger than him, but he wasn't a pushover. Not some fragile omega who would break if I manhandled him.

And oh, how I wanted to manhandle him. But only once I'd earned his complete trust.

Danny slid up my body, his knees on either side of my

hips, and parted his cheeks. Realizing what he wanted, I held my cock straight out from my body as he sank onto it.

I curled toward him, my balls drawing up as I was welcomed into the heated embrace of his hole. We moved together in an easy rhythm until the pleasure got to be too much and I came apart inside him. I pumped his cock and a few seconds later, he spilled onto my belly.

"Mm." I raised my head off the pillow and kissed him. "That's a nice way to wake up."

"My favorite," he murmured, snuggling into my arms.

I held him close, finally able to spare a thought for something other than my cock. I was pretty sure that I was the first alpha he'd been with since his ex, and he'd taken my knot several times now. That had to be wearing on his body.

"How's your ass?" I asked.

He snorted. "Never better."

Was he sure? I bit back the question, knowing he wouldn't appreciate it.

Danny sighed and wiggled against me. "What's wrong?"

I chewed my lip. I didn't want to ruin the moment, but how was I supposed to know where we stood if we didn't talk about it?

"I'm just worried that this is all too much too fast." I shushed him when he immediately protested. "We've been going slow for weeks, and now all of this at once? I don't want you to regret it and pull away from me."

"Oh." To his credit, Danny didn't give a pat response. He paused to consider it before replying. "I can see why you'd worry about that, and I can't promise it won't happen, but I don't think it will."

"Why not?" I smoothed my hands down his back and

breathed in the scents of sex and sweetness. My mate, sticky with our combined release.

"Because the reason we had to go so slow was to build trust." He rested his forearms on either side of me and lifted up to gaze down into my eyes. His eyes were warm, brown, and full of emotions that I'd never seen before. "But you've been good to me, even when it made things harder for you. I trust you."

My heart pounded, and I swallowed, my throat suddenly tight. "You do?"

He hadn't said as much, and I'd assumed it was still a work in progress.

"Yeah." His expression was serene, and so open. He let me see everything going through his mind, not holding any of it back. "I trust you, and I'm done with letting Rex ruin things for me. I want intimacy and closeness, and I want it with you. I love sex, and I want my mate to knot me until I feel him every time I move. Rex doesn't get to hold me back anymore."

I kissed his throat. "I'll knot you as many times as you like. My knot is yours. My heart is yours. Everything I am, body and soul, belongs to you."

Moisture sparkled in his eyes, and when he drew in a breath, it was shaky. "I'm yours, too. I meant it last night, and I still do."

Thank fucking gods.

I nuzzled the crook of his shoulder, my gums itching, my fangs desperate to sink into him, but I restrained myself.

We were together.

We were mates.

But Danny wasn't ready to exchange bites yet, and I wouldn't push him. If I waited, it would mean so much more when he asked me for it.

We lay together until my knot deflated, and then we showered and dressed in clean clothes. Danny insisted on making breakfast for me, and we ate it together on the sofa.

As soon as I'd polished off the last of my meal, Danny set my plate aside and climbed into my lap. He rocked against me, the heady musk of his slick growing stronger.

"Again?" I asked, chuckling. "You're insatiable."

He pouted. "I haven't come from anyone else's touch for months. I deserve to indulge."

I agreed with him. "I've got no problem with that, sweetheart."

He reached for the waistband of his sweatpants, ready to pull them down, but before he had them even halfway over his ass, the doorbell rang.

I covered my face with my hands, my erection never flagging. "Gods damn it."

# THIRTY-SIX

**D**ANNY

"If that's one of my brothers, I'm going to kill whoever it is," I muttered through gritted teeth. Here I was, in the midst of reclaiming my sexuality, and some idiot seemed to think it was a great time to interrupt.

The doorbell rang again, followed by a sharp knock. With a last look at Knox, who was splayed out, his face flushed with desire, his cock straining against his sweatpants and his broad chest heaving deliciously, I clambered off him and straightened.

I tugged my clothes into place, grimacing. My ass was wet, and I didn't want whoever was here to smell my arousal more than they already would, so I dashed to the kitchen and quickly cleaned up before going to the door.

When I undid the lock and opened it, Zander stood on the doorstep. He paused, his nose wrinkled, and he pulled a face. Despite my efforts, the place reeked of sex.

"Why are you here?" I asked, my glower practically daring him to comment.

Zander pressed his lips together and hesitated for a moment. "Sorry for interrupting. Can I... uh... come in?"

Based on how uncomfortable he seemed, I was sure he wouldn't ask if he didn't have a good reason to.

I huffed. "Fine."

I stepped aside to let him in. Knox strode over, and when I glanced down, I noticed that the situation in his pants had resolved itself. Still, there was no mistaking that Zander had caught us at the tail end of an all-night sex-a-thon.

Knox started to offer Zander his hand, then caught himself and shoved it into his pocket. "Any news?"

Zander took a long look at the sofa, then perched on one of the armchairs. "We've had a deputy stationed outside Rex's cabin since yesterday. He hasn't been there."

My gut clenched. I'd been so caught up in our new intimacy that the horrible situation with the dead wolf had temporarily skipped my mind.

"Does that mean he's gone?" I asked hopefully.

Life would be so much easier if Rex decided to leave. I didn't know why he was hanging around here anyway. Certainly no one had treated him like part of the clan since the truth had come out. You didn't beat the Clan Alpha's son and expect to remain welcome.

"It could." Zander didn't sound convinced. "But the deputy looked in through the window and it seems like his stuff is still there. If he'd left the area, he probably would have taken it with him."

"You're right." Knox dropped onto the sofa and patted his knee. I sat on it, drawing comfort from his nearness. "Do we need to worry?"

Worry?

Of course we needed to worry. Someone had killed a

wolf and threatened my mate. Rex had attacked me. Rogue wolves had attempted to kidnap George.

We had plenty to worry about.

"Be on high alert." Zander turned his hat slightly, adjusting it seemingly for the sake of it rather than out of any need to. "Rex could have gone furry for a couple of days. He might reappear once he's cooled down, but the whole thing is suspicious."

"We'll be careful," I promised, relieved that even after Zander left I would have Knox here with me.

"Good." Zander stood. "I'll, uh, let you get back to business."

With a tiny smirk, he let himself out of the house.

I buried my face in Knox's chest and closed my eyes. When would this end?

If only I'd been smart enough to realize that Rex was trouble from the beginning, none of this would be happening. Or at least the stuff with the wolf and the asshole ex wouldn't be.

But no, I'd been taken in by a handsome face and broad shoulders.

"Hey." Knox's chest rumbled beneath my cheek, oddly soothing. "No wallowing."

I tilted my face to look up at him. "I feel like I deserve to wallow a little."

He narrowed his eyes. "Or... we could finish what we were starting before Zander interrupted."

"Uh-uh." I no longer felt remotely sexy.

Although... when Knox rubbed my cock through the fabric of my sweatpants and sucked a bruise onto the side of my neck, maybe a thread of lust pulsed through me.

And when he reached inside my pants and began to tease the head of my cock with the callused pad of his thumb, perhaps I whined and bit my lip to keep from asking for more.

Maybe after that I shoved my pants down, demanded he do the same, and keened when he gathered both of our cocks together in his big, rough hand.

"Oh, gods." I rocked my hips, rubbing against him, the slide exquisite. With each aborted thrust, the head of his cock bumped against mine, and the veins of his girthy shaft drove me as crazy as a ribbed toy.

I threw my head back, whimpering and moaning as he worked us together, his low grunts and groans providing a backing track that would play in my fantasies for years.

He circled my hole with the tip of one of the fingers of his free hand and plunged it inside me. I cried out. He crooked his finger, brushing it over my poor, wrung-out prostate.

I screamed, tears spilling down my cheeks as I emptied all over him. He throbbed against me and gathered up the evidence of our release, wiped it on his shirt, then yanked it off and tossed it aside.

He gathered me against his chest, stroking me and murmuring sweet nothings as though I was a skittish cat.

"It will be okay," he promised, running his hand down the nape of my neck. "Everything will be okay."

I wanted him to be right, but I had a feeling that something very bad was on the horizon, and that when it happened it would be all my fault.

# THIRTY-SEVEN

K NOX
I carried the cardboard box through the Search and Rescue team's headquarters and into the break room. The place was quieter than usual, with only a handful of people present, and the atmosphere was somber.

My colleagues gathered around as I placed the box in the center of the table and opened it.

"Go for it," I said, gesturing at the donuts.

I didn't take any for myself. I wasn't in the mood for something sweet—other than my mate. He'd made me a delicious breakfast burrito this morning. Leaving him had been so hard I wouldn't have managed it if not for him literally pushing me out the bakery door.

"Did you walk Danny to work?"

I glanced at Garrick, who'd asked the question. He was standing to the left of the doorway, his hands in his pockets, waiting for his staff to take their pick of the donuts before he moved in.

"I did." I sighed, feeling a yawning pit in my gut that

wouldn't go away. "I offered to spend the day in the bakery, but he wouldn't hear of it."

It went against all of my instincts to leave him unguarded when we knew that Rex had it out for him and may or may not be killing off wildlife to make a statement.

"He should be safe at work," Garrick said, as reasonably as a man who didn't have a mate and couldn't possibly understand how I felt. "We can drop in a couple of times during the day to check on him."

I cleared my throat. "I've already asked him to message me every hour on the hour."

Was that over the top?

Probably.

Did I care?

Not if it meant that Danny was safe.

Garrick nodded. "Good thinking. Are the donuts from him?"

"Yeah." I wasn't thoughtful enough to bring my work-mates treats without his prompting.

"You don't want any?"

"Sweet stuff isn't my thing."

He laughed. "Don't let Danny hear you say that."

"Okay, I'll rephrase. Danny is the only sweet thing I'll ever need."

He grimaced, looking like he didn't know whether to gag or pat me on the back. He settled for arching an eyebrow and making his way to the now half-empty donut box. He helped himself to a chocolate donut and sauntered out again.

I went to the kitchen counter and fixed myself a cup of instant coffee. Danny had already made me an espresso, but I needed more caffeine.

As the cup filled, I closed my eyes and brought the image of his gorgeous face to the forefront of my mind. I couldn't help but wish that I'd bitten him already, so I could feel a more tangible connection to him. Sure, there was a link of sorts between us, but it was weak and could easily be broken or influenced.

If I bit Danny and bonded with him properly, then I'd know for sure whether he was safe and happy at all times. Unfortunately, I couldn't rush it. He might not be ready for that step for months. I had to be patient.

My coffee overflowed and I cursed, clunking it down on the countertop and hurrying to rinse the hot liquid from my fingers. I wiped down the cup, mopped it up from the counter, and left before I could hurt myself again.

My team was gathered in the open-plan area, seats arranged in a messy semicircle opposite Garrick.

"What did I miss?" I asked, taking the nearest chair.

"Nothing much," Everett said. "We don't have a case, so we were talking over what happened with the wolf, Danny and Rex, and the rogue wolves, and whether it's all connected."

"Huh. And the verdict is?"

"I think it's connected," Francis said, his hands laced together where they rested on his lap. He was the youngest on the team and always in motion. Even now, he was rocking back and forth on his chair. "It's too weird not to be, right?"

Yuri scrunched his face like he didn't agree. He hadn't bothered to tie his hair back today, and it hung in golden locks. "Rex is an asshole. He's always been one. But I don't think he'd associate with anyone as dangerous as the rogue wolf pack. His assholery is on a different level."

Garrick turned to me. "What do you think?"

I shrugged. "I've never met Rex, and I can't say my thoughts are crystal clear where Danny is concerned."

Other than he belonged to me and I'd destroy anyone who tried to come between us.

"Fair enough. What about you?" he asked Angela, the only female team member present this morning.

She finished swallowing a mouthful of donut and brushed crumbs off her black leather pants. "I want to kick Rex's ass, regardless of whether he's involved with the wolves or not. I want to rain hell on them for scaring sweet little Skye and Danny. It makes no difference to me whether the two are connected."

We discussed the matter for a while longer, until a call came in about an older female shifter with dementia who'd gone out for a walk and hadn't returned. Garrick sent Yuri and Francis to handle the matter, and left Everett in charge of the office while he and I took everyone's coffee orders as an excuse to check on Danny.

As we left, Garrick grabbed one of the police radios and hooked it onto his belt. I doubted he was supposed to have it, but since we shared a goal—Danny's continued safety— I didn't say anything about it.

We walked to the bakery and gave Skye the coffee order.

While we were waiting, Danny emerged from out back and stopped in front of me, crossing his arms and tapping his foot.

"I know what you're doing," he said.

I exchanged an innocent glance with Garrick. "Getting coffee?"

Danny rolled his eyes. "You're being a worrywart. Both of you. You don't have to be so anxious. I won't leave the building alone, and my boss has made sure there are two people working all day, so neither of us will be on our own here either."

"So they should," Garrick muttered.

"You matter to us," I told Danny, but I didn't think he

was actually bothered by our meddling. He'd looked grateful when he'd seen us here. He just didn't want us to view him as weak. And I didn't, but that didn't mean I was blind to his vulnerabilities.

His expression softened. "You matter to me, too."

Skye brought our coffees over, and we carried a tray each as we left. Halfway back, voices came over the radio on Garrick's belt.

"Sheriff!" I recognized the voice as Hawk's. "Two people are missing from the Omega House."

CHAPTER

# THIRTY-EIGHT

K*NOX*

My mouth turned dry. Missing omegas?

Garrick juggled his tray of coffee, trying to get to the radio. I took the tray from him, freeing his hands, and he snatched the radio off his belt, raising it to his mouth.

"Knox and I will meet you there," he said.

"Garrick?" It was Zander. "Why are you on this frequency?"

Garrick didn't answer. Nor did I. We legged it back to the station, dumped the coffees in the break room, and rushed out the back door to Garrick's vehicle. The car beeped as he unlocked it with his key fob. I jumped in the passenger side and he slid behind the steering wheel and started the engine.

We arrived at the Omega House at the same time as Zander and Clay. The manager was pacing outside, his hair standing on end as if he'd run his hands through it over and over again.

"They're gone," he cried as we got out of the car. "We have to find them. What if the alphas they were running from came for them? What if they're hurt... or worse?"

207

Garrick went to the man and placed his hand on the back of his neck. Perhaps it was because he was the Clan Alpha's son, or just because he had a reassuring presence, but the manager began to calm down.

I looked over at Hawk, who was standing at the base of the front porch.

"Let's see what Hawk has to report," Zander murmured.

I stuck close behind him and Clay as they approached their colleague. Technically, I had no official reason to be here, but I hoped they wouldn't send me away.

"What do you know?" Zander asked.

Hawk glanced at the manager and then back to Zander. "The two missing omegas are Hannah Warren and Jessie Tate. According to Hamish, he didn't realize they were missing until ten minutes ago when he entered their room. He thought they'd overslept, and since Hannah is a recent addition to the house, he didn't want to disturb her."

"So, Hamish thought they were sleeping but eventually went to make sure they were okay and found them gone?" Zander clarified.

Hawk nodded. "That's correct.

"He's certain they haven't left for a walk or something?"

"He says they have to sign in and out every time they leave the house, and they haven't done that."

"Are the beds disturbed?" I asked, unable to help myself. I pretended not to notice when they all turned to me.

Don't mind me. I'm not here.

"Jessie's bed has been slept in. Hannah's is untouched."

"That's not unusual." The house manager—Hamish, I assumed—had collected himself enough to join the conversation. "When new omegas join us, they often suffer from anxiety and panic attacks. Hannah probably slept with Jessie for comfort."

"I see." Zander's eyes were calculating. "Can you show me the room? Knox, you can come too. I want to know if you can sniff anything out."

Hamish led us inside and down a long hall with faded pink carpet and lined with plain white doors. None of them were labeled, but he knocked once on the fourth one and turned the handle.

Zander went inside first. I leaned against one side of the doorframe, waiting for him to complete his preliminary check.

As he did, I studied the interior myself. The left side of the room was probably Hannah's because the bed was turned down but unused, the nightstand bare except for a cell phone and charger, and her clothes were packed in a duffel bag on the floor.

By contrast, the right side of the room looked homey, with cozy, colorful blankets, clothes strewn about, a stack of books beside the bed, and the trash bin overflowing with chocolate wrappers. Whoever occupied this half was clearly more comfortable in their surroundings, and perhaps more certain of their place here.

Zander looked over his shoulder at me. "Knox."

"Want me to shift?" I asked. I'd pick up more scents in my wolf form.

"Yes, please."

I stripped off, dropping my clothes in the doorway. As my shift rolled over me, I padded to Jessie's bed and sniffed. A bubblegum-sweet scent was embedded in the sheets and pillow. Probably hers. Another scent, crisper and cleaner, like the grass after a rainstorm, was present but less enmeshed. That must belong to Hannah.

I circled the room, breathing in deep lungfuls of every scent present until I found something that didn't quite fit.

It was faint... more of a memory of a scent than a scent itself. Most shifters would never notice it.

I drew in a long, slow breath, pulling more of the scent into my lungs. Still, I couldn't place it.

Frustrated, I shifted back. Hamish tossed me my clothes and I put them on, aware that a large naked alpha might startle the other residents.

"There's a foreign scent," I said as I tugged the T-shirt over my head and shrugged on the jacket. "I can't tell what it is though."

Garrick's eyebrows rose. "But your nose is the best."

I grimaced. "I could be wrong, but I think it's being hidden by something." I hesitated, reluctant to voice my suspicions. "Like, perhaps by a warlock."

Hamish stiffened and his face blanched. Garrick swore.

Zander just adjusted his hat and eyed me curiously. "You think you could follow the foreign scent?"

I chewed the inside of my cheek. "I can try."

I didn't think I'd get anywhere, but it was worth a shot.

"Clay will accompany you."

Clay jerked his head toward the front door and I followed him out. I stripped off again, handed him my clothes, and shifted.

I roamed the grounds, searching for that strange foreign scent with the tiniest hint of ozone that usually signaled the use of magic. It took only seconds to find a trace of it.

I changed back. "Got it. But first, I need to make a call. Can you give me my phone?"

Clay dug into my jeans pocket, withdrew my phone, and passed it to me. I ducked behind a bush, hoping not to startle any passersby with my nudity, and pulled up Danny's number.

When he didn't immediately answer, nerves began to

jangle in my gut, but thankfully his voice came onto the line before I panicked.

"Are you in the bakery?" I asked.

"Yeah." His tone was confused. "Why?"

I lowered my voice. "Two female omegas are missing from the Omega House. We don't know what happened or where they've gone. Please don't go anywhere alone, and pass the message along to Skye, Milo, and any other omegas you see to stay in pairs."

"Oh, my gods. Those poor girls. Are they..." He trailed off, as if too scared to ask for more information.

"There was no blood at the scene." Hopefully that would ease his nerves. "We'll do everything we can to find them. In the meantime, please stay safe."

"I will," he promised. "Good luck."

I came out from behind the bush, passed the phone to Clay, and allowed my wolf to take control.

I found the traces of ozone and bubblegum quickly and began to follow. Clay jogged to keep up. The scent rounded the corner and then vanished.

I growled. Damn it. I'd lost them.

# CHAPTER
# THIRTY-NINE

*DANNY*

My stomach growled and I glanced at the clock on the bakery wall. Time for lunch.

"Are you all good here?" I asked Skye.

Angela, one of the shifters from the Search and Rescue team, had dropped by to watch over us after completing whatever job she'd been on. It was obvious she had a crush on Skye so I was comfortable leaving them together. Angela would never let Skye get hurt.

Skye grinned shyly and snuck a peek at Angela. "Yeah. Do you have someone to walk you home?"

"Milo?"

Milo nodded. He'd turned up not long before Angela had. Melinda and Aaron had been on their way to the Children's Home, and they'd dropped him off to keep an eye on me.

I helped Milo up, and he grimaced, pressing his hand to the small of his back.

"This is going to be a big baby," he complained.

"You're going to be a great Dad," I assured him, twining my arm with his and pushing the bakery door open for him.

After Rex, I'd feared that I'd never trust an alpha enough to have children with them, but I could see that happening with Knox. In fact, it was possible I was already carrying his baby. After all, we'd had unprotected sex.

"Thanks." He flashed me an adorable smile. "I hope so."

We wandered home together, taking it slow because he couldn't do much more than waddle. Our houses were only a short walk down from each other, so I stopped at his doorstep, waited for him to enter and for the lock to click, then I continued the last couple of hundred yards to my own place.

I unlocked the door, took off my shoes, and went inside. As soon as the lock engaged behind me, I relaxed. I padded through the house on bare feet, washed my hands, and made myself a sandwich.

I sat on the sofa to eat and sent Knox a message to ask how it was going. That done, I finished my sandwich and called Momma.

"Hey, honey." Her warm voice wrapped around me like a hug.

"Hi, Momma. How are George and the kids?"

"They're good. Everyone here is safe and staying inside. We've locked all the doors and are prepared to spend the night if needed, although your dad wants to call a clan meeting. I've convinced him to give your brothers a few hours to investigate before he takes over."

"I'm sure they appreciate that." Dad was a great Clan Alpha, but Grizzly Ridge was a mostly peaceful place to live and rescue operations were certainly not his forte, while my brothers had been trained for it.

"You're still at the bakery?" she asked.

Holding the phone to my ear with one hand, I used the other to carry my empty plate to the kitchen and slot it into the dishwasher.

"I'm at home. Milo and I walked back together."

"You're alone?" The question was sharp.

"Yes, while locked inside my house."

She made a sound of distress. "Danny, I really don't think that's the best idea. Perhaps you should join Milo at his place."

I pursed my lips, trying to ignore a flicker of discomfort. She was probably right. I'd thought that walking Milo safely home would be enough, but he was pregnant and not a shifter. I shouldn't have left him on his own.

"I'll go there now. Talk soon."

"Love you."

I hung up and tried Milo's number.

"Hello?" he asked sleepily. I must have woken him from a nap.

"Hey, Milo. I'm coming over. Is that all right?"

"Sure." He yawned. "Knock five times and I'll let you in."

"Be there in a minute."

I ended the call and pocketed my phone, then looked around to make sure I hadn't forgotten anything. I switched the light off and hurried to the door, bending to pick up my shoes.

A faint bump of wood against something solid came from outside.

I froze.

For a long moment, all was silent, and I began to think I was hearing things, but then one of the floorboards on the porch creaked beneath a person's weight and my breath caught.

Someone was out there.

I was tempted to call out. Surely it was just one of my family members, or perhaps another neighbor, but as I remained perfectly still for several seconds and there was no knock on the door, I realized that it couldn't be.

Slowly, the door handle turned.

I backtracked, almost stumbling over myself in my haste to get away. I put the shoe down and, as quietly as possible, made my way through the house, keeping low so that no one would see me through the windows.

I'd almost reached the back door when a stone skittered across the ground outside. If I wasn't so attuned to everything around me, I might not have heard it.

But I did.

Not only was someone trying to get into the front of the house, but a second person was sneaking around the back.

My head spun and black spots appeared in my vision.

I was hyperventilating.

How was I supposed to get out of here? I was trapped between two people. There were no other doors. If whoever was here meant me harm, I was a sitting duck.

ANNY

Okay, okay, get it together, Danny.

My pulse thumped erratically at the base of my throat and I tiptoed away from the door, moving quietly in the hopes that whoever was there wouldn't hear me.

Plastering myself against the wall, I inhaled slowly, doing my best to both calm myself and scent the unwelcome guests. I could detect traces of the nearest person and knew that they were an alpha, male, and possessed the faint doggy aroma of a wolf shifter.

It wasn't someone I knew.

Gods, was this one of the rogue wolves from Moonlight Cove that I'd heard so much about? Had they come to kidnap me as well as those poor women from the Omega House?

But why?

I understood attacking the Omega House. They'd know that there were a number of omegas inside who were unprotected by alphas. It made no sense to come after me though. I was a higher-risk target. Perhaps they thought it would be worth it because I was the Clan Alpha's son.

I tiptoed down the hall and into my bedroom, praying to every god I knew that the intruders wouldn't hear me. I dropped to my knees, aware that they'd be able to see me through the window otherwise, and crawled to the night-stand, reaching for the handle of the top drawer. I inched it open and felt around for the small handgun that Knox had insisted on leaving there in case I ever needed it for protection.

I'd thought he was being paranoid, but now I was grateful to him.

Carefully, quietly, I checked that it was loaded and turned off the safety. Keeping the gun aimed away from me, I crawled across the room to the window and stealthily rose to my feet, pressed flat to the wall. I switched the gun from my right hand to my left and reached across to unlatch the window. I grabbed the bottom and began to lift.

It creaked.

I snatched my hand back, my heart thumping rapidly while I waited to see whether either of the intruders had heard the noise. When no one came and there was a bang at the front door, I eased the window farther up until there was enough room for me to slip through.

I peeked outside. I didn't see anyone, so perhaps I'd have time to make a run for it. If I shifted as soon as I hit the ground, I'd stand a decent chance of getting away. A bear couldn't outrun a wolf, but all I'd need to do was escape for long enough to attract help.

I stripped off, keeping hold of the gun and straining my ears for the slightest sound. I looked outside again.

The coast was clear.

I flicked the safety back into place and slid through the window, landing softly on the grass. I set the gun down while I shifted. Fur sprouted, my nose elongated, and my frame bulked up. Scents became stronger, sounds clearer.

I ducked my head to pick up the gun with my mouth, but before I could grasp it properly, a man came around the corner of the house and put himself between me and my avenue of escape.

There was a laugh from behind me.

"Looks like we're just in time."

I whipped my head around. Another alpha stood at the other end of the house. Both men were tall and rangy, with harsh features and hungry eyes. I fought the urge to cower. They didn't look like they'd think twice about hurting me.

"What were you planning to do with that gun, little bear?" the alpha nearest the road teased. "You can't shoot it with your mouth."

I glanced between them, not sure which one to keep my eyes on, but afraid to look away from either.

I should never have left the bakery.

I definitely shouldn't have left Milo alone. Although, perhaps if I'd stayed with him then we'd both be in danger. At least this way, he might be safe. Gods, I hoped they hadn't sent other wolves to kidnap him. I'd never forgive myself if they did.

"Come here, little bear," the wolf called, his voice high and falsely sweet.

Adrenaline pumped through me, but I couldn't summon a single clear thought.

What should I do?

I could try to shift back and use the gun, but shifting would take a precious few seconds and I'd put the safety in place, so they might rush me before I was able to use it. Even if I was fast enough, I'd never shot at someone before. There was every chance I wouldn't hit them, or that if I did, it would only be a graze.

I stepped away from the gun. It was too risky.

Instead, I turned toward the wolf shifter who'd put

himself between me and my escape route, and I charged him.

His eyes widened, and for a moment I thought I'd get past him, but then something stung my chest and the world started to go black at the edges.

I crashed to the ground, feeling myself return to my human form. I tried to struggle as I was hefted roughly over someone's shoulder, carried a short distance, and dumped on a gritty vinyl floor, but my efforts did nothing to stop them.

Then everything faded out.

CHAPTER

# FORTY-ONE

K*NOX*

I shifted restlessly on the hard chair, eager to stop fucking chatting and take action. We weren't any closer to finding Hannah and Jessie than we had been an hour ago, but Zander insisted on holding a goddamn meeting.

"...while we instigate a perimeter search of—"

"Sheriff!" The receptionist barged into the bullpen, reeking of distress. Her eyes were wide, her pulse racing, and her face was an unusual shade of burgundy.

Zander stood, unflustered by the interruption. "What is it, Nell?"

She took so long to respond that I wanted to shake it out of her. Clearly, something was very wrong.

"There are another two missing omegas," she panted, looking as though she might faint. "The calls just came in. They didn't return to work after lunch, and a white van was reported speeding through the center of town and driving dangerously."

"We're sure the omegas are missing and not just staying home with their families until the danger blows over?"

220

Zander asked. It was a smart question. I wasn't sure I'd have thought to raise it.

Nell shook her head. "I've checked. They aren't at home either. I think..." She bit her lip. "Sir, I have a really bad feeling about this."

So did I, and my instincts didn't often steer me wrong.

"Get me their details," Zander said.

"Yes, sheriff." She hurried out.

The room fell silent. No one seemed inclined to speak. I noticed Everett on his phone and wondered if he was messaging Milo to check in. I should do the same with Danny. I pulled my phone from my pocket, but before I had the chance to type anything, Nell rushed back into the room, even more purple than before.

"It's happened again!" she cried. "Jamie Burke was taking his mother to a medical appointment when they were attacked and he was snatched off the street."

"Fuck," I swore. "What about his mother?" If I recalled correctly, she was the same person we'd already been charged with finding once today. She wasn't fully aware of what was going on around her, and there was no telling what she might have done if attacked.

"The doctors have her." Nell wrung her hands. "But Jamie... that poor boy..."

Zander narrowed his eyes in thought. "Deputies Clay, Hawk, and Bea, I want each of you to take the lead on one of the missing omegas. Nell will provide names. Talk to their family, bosses, colleagues, and friends. Find out if anyone saw anything. Someone needs to talk to Mrs. Burke and the doctor ASAP to see if they got a description of the attacker."

"Z." Garrick jerked his head toward his own team.

Zander nodded. "Deputies, I want you to each partner with someone from Search and Rescue. There's a chance we'll be able to trace them from one of the crime scenes, although it seems they have a warlock helping to cover their tracks."

Garrick ordered Angela, Yuri, and Francis to accompany the deputies.

Once they were gone, Zander addressed those of us who remained. "I have to wonder whether the first kidnapping —that of Hannah and Jessie—was intended to distract us while additional kidnappings were undertaken."

"Surely they'd know we'd be on guard if there had been a kidnapping," I pointed out.

He shrugged one shoulder. "Perhaps, but they'd also know that our resources would be occupied. We're a small town; we only have so many people available to help."

I gritted my teeth, knowing he was right even though I hated it. I finished tapping out a message to Danny and sent it. Almost immediately, Zander's phone rang.

"Sheriff Blackwood," he answered, raising the phone to his ear without checking the screen. "Hold on. Calm down, Milo. What did you say?"

I stiffened. Everett was already on his feet, his eyes a brilliant gold.

"Danny was taken?" Zander asked.

Fear lanced through me. My fangs extended, catching on my lower lip, and I growled.

*No, no, no.*

It wasn't possible. Danny was safe at the bakery. He'd promised not to go anywhere alone.

Zander glanced at me and turned away, speaking more softly into the phone although he must realize that I could hear every word. He ended the call and pocketed his phone, pivoting slowly toward us. His face was pale, his eyes shimmering unnaturally. It might be the most emotion I'd ever seen him display.

"Milo and Danny walked home for lunch together.

Danny told Milo he was on his way back to see him but didn't show. Milo went over to check on him, and he said it looked as though he might have been taken."

A growl tore through me. Fur rippled across the exposed skin of my forearms, and I snarled.

This couldn't be happening.

I should never have left the bakery earlier. I should have spent the day parked inside, refusing to leave no matter what else happened.

I'd let my mate down.

"What about Milo?" Everett asked.

"He called Dad to come and get him. He was just arriving as we ended the call."

Everett relaxed slightly but then tensed again, as if recalling that his brother was still in danger. "Are we sure it was the wolves? It could have been Rex."

I growled again, my hands curling into claws. If that asshole laid so much as a finger on Danny, he would pay for it.

"One way to find out." Zander gestured to the door. "Everett and Knox, go. See what you can find. You'd both be useless here anyway."

I grabbed my jacket from over the back of the chair and shoved my arms into it, all of my instincts driving me to get my eyes on Danny as quickly as possible.

"Car?" Everett asked.

"Yeah." If we had to drive anywhere from Danny's place, it would be faster to have transportation already with us.

We hurried out and got into the car, then drove over. Aaron's vehicle was parked outside and he, Milo, and Melinda were all inside. We pulled up behind them and I threw the door open and jumped out before the engine was even off.

I paused, sniffing, but there was no scent except for the faintest hint of wolf and ozone. The warlock was getting better at masking their presence.

I headed to the front door and tried the handle. It was locked, so I inserted my key and let myself in. The living area smelled of both Danny and myself and there were no foreign scents, thank gods.

In the hall, his sweet scent turned sour with fear. My chest constricted, and I flexed my hands, ready to fight to defend my mate.

Only... I was too late.

I followed the scent of terror to the back door and then to the bedroom. The window was ajar. I climbed through and dropped to the ground. The gun I'd left in Danny's nightstand lay discarded on the grass.

"He came out this way," I called.

Knox jogged around the corner. Aaron didn't follow, which surprised me. He must have decided to stay out in front to protect Milo and Melinda if needed.

"They trapped him in the house, so he tried to escape through the window." I nudged the gun with my foot. "He was prepared to defend himself, but it doesn't look like he got the chance. I don't know about you, but I don't smell any blood."

That was a relief, at least. If they'd killed him, he would have bled. Shifters didn't slaughter their enemies neatly.

I stripped off, ignoring the chill in the air, and my wolf took over. We followed Danny's scent to the edge of the property and onto the road, where it came to an abrupt halt.

Damn.

I closed my eyes and groped around, searching for the weak connection between us. It wasn't fully formed yet, but it should be enough to lead me to him. My consciousness grabbed onto the bond and began to follow it. But a few yards away it was as if I ran into a brick wall, beyond which my sense of the bond vanished.

Shit. The warlock had messed with my ability to find my mate. I just prayed it was more of their masking magic and that they hadn't damaged our bond. Surely I'd have felt it if they had. Wouldn't I?

# FORTY-TWO

*D*ANNY

My face ached. My head throbbed. My ribs felt too tight.

I blinked, but despite my open eyes, I couldn't see anything.

Panic rose within me. Was I blind?

I sat up, and everything spun.

"Whoa. Take it easy." A soft touch landed on my shoulder. "Don't move too fast. Give your eyes a chance to adjust to the dark."

It was a woman's voice. Vaguely familiar, but not enough for me to recognize it.

"Where am I?" I asked.

The last thing I remembered, I'd been charging at the rogue wolf shifter.

"I'm not sure. It might be a basement." She moved closer, and I realized she was crouched beside me.

I turned toward her. A strip of light shone from beneath a door at the top of a flight of stairs, illuminating her features well enough for me to make out braided dark hair, dark skin, and dark, gleaming eyes.

"Who are you?" I asked.

"I'm Jessie. I live in Grizzly Ridge. You do too, right? I've seen you in the bakery." She spoke in hushed tones, glancing behind herself as if worried that someone on the other side of the door might overhear us.

"Yeah." I scanned the room. I didn't dare let my bear come to the surface so I could see better just in case Jessie wasn't a shifter, but even with my limited human vision, I could make out several other figures in the room.

There was a woman rocking in the corner, with long, pale hair that spilled over her arms as she hugged her knees and sobbed. Five figures lay prone on the concrete floor, although one was beginning to stir.

"You were kidnapped?" I asked quietly. It seemed obvious, but it was best to be sure.

She nodded. "Men came in the middle of the night. They drugged us before we woke up, so I only pieced together what happened after we arrived here." She gestured to the sobbing woman. "Hannah and I have been here for hours. The rest of you arrived maybe half an hour ago."

"Thanks, Jessie." I tried to stand, but my legs were too wobbly, so instead I dragged myself over to the person who was in the midst of regaining consciousness. "Hello?"

"Danny?"

My gut clenched. "Jamie?"

"Yeah." He rubbed his eyes, then hissed. When I looked closer, I realized that the left one had been blackened. "What's going on?"

Jessie had joined us, so I waited for her to repeat everything she'd told me. As subtly as possible, I sniffed, hoping I'd be able to detect how many people were upstairs and whether or not they were all shifters.

Unfortunately, all I could smell was damp and mold.

Jessie patted my back and indicated that she was going to comfort Hannah. Meanwhile, Jamie and I checked the other four, but they were all still out of it. One of them was a shifter, but the others weren't. Perhaps whatever they'd dosed us with had longer-lasting effects on humans.

"How did they get you?" I asked Jamie.

All of a sudden, his heart rate picked up. "Oh, gods. Mom!"

"What is it?"

The whites of his eyes showed in the dim light. "I was taking Mom to an appointment. We'd just parked when they attacked. What if they hurt her?"

My stomach knotted. Now I understood his concern.

"I'm sure they didn't," I soothed, even though I was absolutely not sure of anything. "She's not here, and they wouldn't have any use for a sick omega, right?"

Jamie didn't seem consoled by this, and I didn't blame him.

One of the others began to rouse, and I made my way over to help ease her panic as we waited for the rest of our companions to come around.

They woke soon after, and another fifteen minutes or so after that, the door at the top of the stairs opened and a pair of wolves appeared, silhouetted against the light. One of them flicked a light switch, illuminating the basement so rapidly that I had to shield my eyes.

Hannah cried out, and Jessie shushed her.

The larger of the two wolves swaggered down the stairs, his long ratty hair loose around his shoulders.

"Welcome. This is my packhouse and while you're here, my word is law. You're my omegas now, under my leadership, and you will do what I say."

"Or what?" Jessie asked, her tone challenging.

The guy—the Pack Alpha, I assumed—laughed. "Or

what, she asks? Or things are going to be really shitty for you, darling." He clapped his hands. "So, raise your hand if you have a useful skill? Like if you can cook, mend clothing, or if you're a nurse... blah blah blah. Basically, I want to know if you can be useful to us."

No one moved.

He sighed. "I'll give you a couple of hours to think about it. Anyone who has no practical use will become a plaything for my men, and trust me, they aren't gentle with their toys."

Bile churned up the back of my throat, but I swallowed it down. I was immediately tempted to announce that I was a pastry chef, but I wasn't going to play their games. We wouldn't be here for long anyway. My family would rescue us. Right?

"You." The Pack Alpha pointed at me. "Come here."

Fear glued my bare feet to the ground. "No."

With a huff, he gestured to the guy behind him, who marched toward me, already reaching out.

I tried to shift.

I called on my bear with everything I had, but he didn't respond.

Terror seized me, making it difficult to breathe. What had they done to me?

The wolf grabbed my arm and yanked me toward the stairs. I stumbled but caught myself before I fell.

My heart hammered. I didn't know whether to fight to stay with the other omegas, or whether to go with them in the hopes that they might give me the opportunity to escape and find help.

In the end, I didn't have much choice. The wolf was stronger than me. He hauled me up the stairs and tossed me into a room to the left of the basement doorway. Before

I had a chance to react, he slammed the door and the lock snicked shut, plunging the room into darkness.

I placed my hands against the door and felt around for the handle. I tried it, but as expected, it was locked. I moved around, feeling my way along the wall, careful of where I put my feet in case I tripped over anything.

It took less than a minute to conduct a full circuit of the room. It must be a cleaning closet of some sort because it was small, with what felt like a mop and a bucket stashed in one corner, and it reeked of bleach.

There were no windows and, as far as I could tell, nothing other than the mop handle that could be used as a weapon. Honestly, I didn't like my odds of doing much damage with the mop handle either. Nevertheless, I removed the end of the mop and kept the handle close by in case an opportunity presented itself.

Now that I'd determined where I was, I sat in the back corner and focused on any noises filtering in from beyond the closet.

Unfortunately, there were none.

Perhaps no one was here, or they were being quiet, but the wolves I'd seen didn't strike me as the type to stay silent. More likely, the warlock that was working with them had erected a ward to keep their conversations private.

I closed my eyes and breathed deeply. Panicking wouldn't do me any good, but it was hard not to when I was trapped by myself in a tiny space and no one knew where I was.

Gods, if only I'd mated properly with Knox. Then he'd have been able to find me anywhere and I wouldn't feel so damned alone. I mean, there was a possibility he'd be able to find me anyway, but the more distance between us the more difficult it would be for him to hunt me down.

Tears sprang to my eyes. It would have been so reassuring to be able to bask in the certainty of that connection now. Why had I been so stubborn in putting off our mating?

I stood and shook myself.

Okay, I wasn't going to sit here like a lamb waiting for slaughter.

First, I called forth my bear. Once again, he didn't respond. It was as if he was sleeping somewhere in the back of my consciousness.

All right, so shifting wasn't an option. I was still strong. Perhaps I could knock down the door.

I geared up, ready to charge, but just before I launched forward the handle turned, and a familiar scent filled my nostrils.

Bitter coffee.

My insides turned cold.

Rex entered, and I backed up against the wall, tripping over the bucket.

He grinned. "Hello, Danny."

## CHAPTER
# FORTY-THREE

K*NOX*

"They're ahead of us because they have a warlock," I growled as I paced from one side of the bullpen to the other. "What we need is a warlock of our own that knows tracking spells."

Garrick leaned back in his chair, his knees spread wide; only the lines of tension on his forehead gave away how stressed he was. "We don't have anyone with that capability in Grizzly Ridge."

Zander rose, his clothes rustling, his hat slightly askew. "I'll make some calls. There are some warlocks who work with law enforcement. Perhaps we can get one to help us out."

"Do it," I said.

The brothers exchanged a look, as if silently debating whether to call me on the fact that they were both more senior than me and couldn't be bossed around, but they must have decided not to because neither of them spoke. Zander withdrew his phone from his pocket and strode into one of the private meeting rooms.

While we waited to find out whether he'd have any

luck, Garrick and Everett continued putting together a plan for a grid search of Moonlight Cove. Zander had liaised with their sheriff's department, but to no one's surprise, they were unwilling to help because the rogue pack had a reputation for killing those who stood against them.

On the opposite side of the bullpen, Deputy Bea—I'd yet to learn whether that was a first or last name—was putting her criminal psychology degree to good use to search for commonalities between the omegas that we knew had been taken.

I just sat there. Useless.

I should be doing something. Searching, gathering information, torturing anyone who might have useful knowledge to share. I'd wanted to drive straight into Moonlight Cove and search for the packhouse. It was a relatively small town, so I was sure it wouldn't take long to find it.

But Aaron had ordered me not to.

The more time passed, the more I wondered if it might be worth defying him. My mate's life was on the line.

Growling, I raked my hands down my face, but winced when a claw caught on my upper lip. I was so worried I couldn't even control my goddamn shifts. Without my nose to guide me, I really was of no use to anyone.

The meeting room door opened and Zander stepped out.

I straightened. "Have you found someone?"

He shook his head, his expression grim. "All of the ones we usually work with are already assigned to other cases. There's nobody available."

"Fuck." There had to be someone else. Warlocks weren't that common, but they weren't rare either.

Hold on.

My heart skipped.

I knew a warlock. One who'd cared enough about me to

go against her Pack Alpha's orders at least once. Yes, when my father announced my exile, all of his pack members were forbidden from engaging with me, but Danny's life was at stake. It was worth a shot.

"I'll keep trying." Zander was tapping away on his phone screen. "Maybe there's someone who can come in tomorrow, or later in the week."

"That's not fast enough," I said. "We're going to have them back before then."

There was no other option. I wouldn't allow it.

Zander looked up. "It's better than what we have now."

Which was a big fat nothing.

"I… I might know someone. I'm not supposed to talk to her though."

Zander arched an eyebrow. "Says who?"

"My former Pack Alpha." I swallowed, my throat dry. "My father."

Surprise flickered across Zander's face, but he didn't outwardly react other than that. "Are you willing to take the risk?"

"Yes." I'd do anything for Danny.

I fished my phone from my pocket and scrolled through my contacts until I found her number, labeled with a simple M. My finger hovered above it for two slow seconds, and then I hit the Call button.

"You better be dying." Morag's voice rasped like she'd been smoking two packs of cigarettes a day for thirty years. Knowing her, she probably had.

I drew in a deep breath. I couldn't screw this up. "I'm not, but if I don't save him soon, my mate might be."

"Mate?" She sounded surprised—as she should, since lone wolves often passed their entire lives without finding their mate.

"He's a bear shifter. His name is Danny, and he's been

kidnapped by a rogue wolf pack, along with several other omegas from the town we live in."

Morag sighed. "Please don't tell me they're trafficking omegas."

"I'm pretty sure they are." My chest twinged. "Either for their own use, for profit, or both."

"Shit." She huffed. "Let me guess: you want help to find him."

"Yeah." I wouldn't insult her intelligence by suggesting otherwise.

"Fine." Something rustled. "But after this, you lose my number. Permanently. Got it?"

"I'll delete it as soon as he's home safe and sound."

"You'd better."

"You have my word. What do you need for the spell?"

She hummed in thought. "A photo of him. Something that belonged to him would be better, but the photo will do the trick. I'll also need an approximate location, narrowed to a twenty-mile radius. I could start at a larger scale, but it will take longer."

I turned to Garrick, only to find him and Everett watching me intently. "Do we have a twenty-mile search radius?"

He nodded.

"Done," I told Morag. "Anything else?"

"A few herbs, but I have those here. I'll get set up while you send me the search area and the photo. Stay on the line. I want this over with as quickly as possible. If your father finds out you've called, it'll be Armageddon here."

I grimaced. "I'm sorry. If there had been another way..."

She snorted, and I could picture her rolling her eyes. "I know how you shifters are with your mates. Don't worry, we'll find him."

I switched the phone to speaker and relayed what she'd

said to the others. I gave Garrick her phone number so he could send her a photo of the area they'd been preparing to grid search as a first priority.

While he did that, I searched my phone for a photo of Danny. I'd snapped several over the past weeks. When I found a good one, I sent it to her.

We gathered around the phone. Morag had returned and she was explaining what she was doing since none of us could see. Once she'd arranged everything as necessary, she warned us to remain silent as she began the spell. We practically held our breath as she chanted in a dead language. Then all was quiet.

"I have a location," she announced, kickstarting my heart. "Forty-seven Weyward Crescent, Moonlight Cove."

"Thank you."

She harrumphed. "Lose my number, kid. Good luck."

# CHAPTER
# FORTY-FOUR

*D*ANNY

"A deal is a deal." The Pack Alpha's voice came from behind Rex. "You held up your end and helped us with supplies and the omegas, so now he's all yours and we're square. Your petty vendetta shit is your problem. We're not killing anymore wolves or smashing windows for you. Capisce?"

"Yeah, whatever." Rex didn't sound like he cared what the Pack Alpha said. All of his attention was focused on me.

I dropped to the floor and drew my knees to my chest, scooting backward until I was pressed into the corner.

Still, Rex advanced.

He looked like a bear who'd just discovered a honeycomb. Smug. Self-satisfied. Like he knew he'd already won.

"I'm not going anywhere with you." I raised my chin defiantly. "I won't move from this spot."

Rex folded his arms across his chest. "It's done. Either you can come nicely, or you can get a beating. It doesn't bother me either way."

"I'm not coming," I repeated, curling in on myself

defensively. Once again, I searched within myself for my bear, but he was beyond my reach.

Rex looked at his wolf companion, as if expecting him to step in, but the wolf backed out of the room.

"I'll leave you to it," he said.

Rex's jaw tightened. If I weren't so finely attuned to reading his moods, I might not have noticed, but to me, it was as obvious as a sky-written message.

He stalked toward me, moving slowly and warily but without pause. Then, in one quick motion, he reached over, grabbed me by the collar, and yanked me out of the corner. I lashed out, kicking his leg. I aimed at his knee but missed.

He slammed me back against the wall, forcing the air from my lungs. My head knocked on the concrete and stars appeared in my vision. I gasped, struggling to breathe. Something warm trickled down the side of my face, and I instinctively tried to swipe at it, but Rex grabbed my wrist and stopped me. I planted the bottom of my foot on his gut and pushed, hoping to drive him backward and give myself some room to get away. He grimaced but didn't flinch, so I aimed lower.

His eyes bulged, and his grip on me slackened. I dropped from his grasp and bolted for the door, which the wolf had left ajar. He thudded into me from behind, tackling me to the floor.

I went down hard, and cried out as pain ricocheted through me. One of his hands came across my mouth and I bit down, tasting blood. He swore and yanked it away. I gulped in a lungful of air and screamed as loud as I could. Rex reared back, his sensitive shifter ears desperate to avoid the aural assault.

The door was shoved open, and it whacked into the side of my head. I whimpered, wanting to cover my head to protect it, but with Rex on top of me, I couldn't move my arms.

"What the fuck is going on in here?" the Pack Alpha demanded. "Tie him the fuck up and get him out of here. You're upsetting Reid, and there's only so much I can do to keep him calm. We need him under control for the move or all those supplies we've spent weeks gathering might fucking explode or something if he has a meltdown."

"Help me tie him," Rex grunted. "Then I'll get out of your way. There are zip ties in my pocket."

Someone made a sound of disgust and then two other sets of hands grabbed me. I fought them, but there was nothing I could do as they forced my hands behind my back and pulled a zip tie uncomfortably tight around my wrists.

Rex got off me and grabbed a handful of my hair. He pulled, and I jumped to my feet, doing my best not to trip and fall. He marched out of the room and I staggered behind him, knowing I ought to look around for details I could share with a rescue crew but unable to concentrate on anything other than the burning pain in my scalp.

One of the wolves opened the front door and I blinked, stunned by the brightness. In my mind, I'd thought it would be night by now, but it must still be afternoon or early evening.

A car was parked out the front. Rex opened the back door with his free hand and shoved me toward it. I face-planted on the seat, unable to catch myself with my hands tied behind my back. He crammed my lower legs inside and shut the door.

I wormed forward and bit the door handle on the opposite side, ignoring the pain in my jaw as I pulled it toward myself. The door didn't open. I scanned the interior and my stomach dropped. There was a child lock in place.

Changing tack, I pushed the window button down with

my chin. Again, nothing happened. He must have it set so that only the driver could operate the windows.

Damn it.

As Rex got into the driver's seat, I tried to maneuver myself into position to headbutt him. It was the only thing I could think of that might incapacitate him. Unfortunately, it took too long for me to lever myself into an upright position, and by then, he'd already started the engine.

"Don't try anything." He gestured at something on the front seat. I craned my neck and realized that it was a tranquilizer gun. "I'll drug you again if you do."

Defeated, I collapsed onto the back seat and rested my head against the window as he pulled out and began driving. The vibrations from the engine thrummed through my aching head. Cringing, I moved away from the window and watched the houses pass by.

After only a few minutes, we were out of Moonlight Cove and heading in the direction of Grizzly Ridge.

"Where are you taking me?" I asked, not really expecting him to answer.

"I had a new cabin built midway between here and Grizzly Ridge." He kept his gaze on the road, as if it wasn't worth his time to glance back at me. "It's been outfitted with a basement that has everything I need to keep you the way you deserve to be kept."

My gut clenched, and I leaned forward and heaved the contents of my stomach onto the floor, filling the vehicle with the sour pang of vomit.

He'd had a prison built for me?

I retched again, but flinched backward when Rex swore and smacked at me.

*Please, Knox. Find me soon.*

# FORTY-FIVE

K*NOX*

We parked a couple of streets over, shifted into our animal forms, and made our way on foot to the address Morag had given us. The sun was starting to go down, providing plenty of shadows for us to cling to as we crept up on the enemy.

Aaron was in front. Despite the fact this was a kidnapping, he was taking the lead because it was a shifter matter. His enforcers and the search and rescue team were providing backup for the local police rather than calling in more cops from out of town. We could hardly explain to human officers why they would be facing down a pack of wolves rather than a group of men.

A cold breeze ruffled my fur. I raised my nose and sniffed, instinctively seeking Danny's scent, but of course it was absent, as was the faint thread that used to connect us. The warlock's protective measures must still be in place.

My sharp eyes read the number forty-seven on a mailbox ahead of us. The house it belonged to was a squat building, with off-white plaster-cast walls—most likely with concrete beneath—perched on a patch of dirt with absolutely nothing growing on it, as if the ground itself was tainted.

I bit back a whine as Aaron and Zander's silhouettes morphed from bears to men. I wanted to be with them as they approached the door, but as the Clan Alpha and the sheriff, they were better placed to open negotiations.

I just didn't like it. What if Danny was inside and needed me?

Aaron rapped sharply on the door. We remained farther back, hopefully out of sight, although they'd be able to smell us if they tried. Hopefully, by the time they realized we were here it would be too late.

Zander wanted to do this peacefully, but if any of these wolves had harmed Danny, they wouldn't leave here alive.

The door opened to reveal a guy with long, ratty hair and a build similar to mine. I sniffed. His scent was familiar. He'd been at Danny's house. This was one of the men who'd taken him.

Aaron offered the wolf his hand, but the wolf didn't accept it.

"I'm Clan Alpha Aaron Blackwood of the Grizzly Ridge Clan." Aaron spoke loudly and clearly, his hand still extended. "I'm here to negotiate the peaceful return of our omegas."

The wolf laughed in his face. "We won't be returning anyone, and a backwoods clan like you can't make us."

Zander stepped forward. "I'm Sheriff Blackwood. The kidnapping of seven Grizzly Ridge omegas has been reported to law enforcement and legal action will follow unless you give them up."

The wolf rolled his eyes. "I'm Trent, the Pack Alpha, and on behalf of the Red Moon Pack, fuck you."

He started to slam the door, but Aaron slammed his palm into it and held it open. Zander stepped aside, fur already sprouting over his body, and signaled for us to move.

We raced forward, claws out, snarling and growling, ready to tear flesh from bone to rescue our omegas.

Garrick led the charge, as previously agreed, but I kept pace with him, staying at his shoulder as Trent's eyes widened and he pushed harder, desperate now to shut the door.

"Reid!" Trent shouted, glancing over his shoulder. "Where are the fucking wards?"

His split-second distraction was all it took for Garrick to hit the door and smash it inward, ripping it from the hinges and bowling both the door and Trent to the floor. I rushed past them, scanning the interior of the house for any sign of Danny.

I sniffed and caught a hint of his scent. The warlock must not have bothered to maintain the masking spell within their home.

I also smelled blood.

Fury scorched through my bloodstream. If anyone here had hurt my precious omega, I'd burn them all to the fucking ground.

The rest of the pack had realized they'd been invaded and were spilling through the doorways, either already shifted or in the midst of the change. I couldn't see any omegas—not ours or theirs.

Behind me there was a crash, and Garrick grunted as Trent threw the door off himself and bolted behind his wolves for cover while he shifted.

A wolf leaped at me. I tossed them off. They came back around and swiped at my side. I felt a burn as they broke the skin, and my fury grew. I tussled with them, ignoring the wound on my side until they were pinned beneath me. Then, without hesitation, I tore out their throat.

I looked up, expecting the rest of the pack to have taken this as a warning, but instead, all hell had broken loose. Bears, mountain lions, and other predatory shifters from the Grizzly Ridge Clan were engaged in a bloodthirsty battle with the wolves of the Red Moon Pack.

Blood splattered the floor and walls. At least two wolves lay dead. A mountain lion cried out and a bear swatted the wolf that was attacking them and sheltered them until they picked themself back up.

I scanned the carnage, searching for Trent. Perhaps if we killed him the others would stop resisting. I found him slinking along the back wall, nudging the only person in the room who was still in a two-legged form.

The warlock.

At least, I assumed he must be the warlock given the fact that small blue sparks danced around his hands. He was smaller than I'd expected. An omega, with loose blond curls, cherubic cheeks, and bright blue eyes that were wide with terror.

Trent growled and shoved the warlock with his nose. The warlock raised his hands and sent a shower of blue sparks at the bear I recognized as Aaron. Aaron roared in pain and shied away from them.

The warlock glanced at one of the doors, as if he wanted to make a run for it. Even from here, I could smell his fear. There was nothing as repugnant to an alpha as a scared omega.

Or at least, not to a decent alpha. I doubted any of the Red Moon alphas cared about his distress.

I howled and sprang toward Trent. He was a large wolf with shaggy gray fur and myriad scars, but I wasn't much smaller, and I was a hell of a lot angrier.

He spotted me at the last minute and we collided in a flurry of claws, teeth, and fur. I snapped at him, trying to sink my teeth into his throat, but he hadn't gotten to his position by being a bad fighter and he slashed at me viciously.

Light appeared on the edge of my vision and the smell of singed fur filled my nostrils.

Fuck. The warlock was attacking me.

He sent another shower of sparks at me, and I dodged them and dug my claws into Trent's shoulder. Out of the corner of my eye, I saw Clay bowl the little warlock over and I took advantage of the reprieve to go after Trent with renewed zeal, backing him into a corner.

His gaze darted around, looking for an escape route. Seeing none, he flew at me. I moved to the side just enough to avoid the brunt of the attack, then sideswiped him and, without any finesse, rolled him to the floor and tore at his throat until it was shredded and beyond healing.

Trent returned to human form as he died.

I howled, alerting my clan to the fact I'd taken out the Pack Alpha. Around me, the action stilled.

Then a scream pierced the air. A haunting, terrible, grief-stricken scream. The warlock blasted Clay off him and threw himself on Trent's body, wailing and sobbing, clutching the man's shoulders and trying desperately to revive him.

It was only then that I noticed the bite mark at the base of his neck.

Fuck. The warlock was Trent's mate.

He reared back and another scream tore through him. Light blazed around him, and the hairs on the back of my neck stood up.

Oh, shit.

Magic pulsed in the air. It spread from the young man, glowing a brilliant orange. I had a sinking feeling that I'd chosen to go after the wrong person. Trent hadn't been the most dangerous creature in this house.

His mate was.

It wasn't too late though.

I pounced on the warlock, knocking him off his feet. The orange glow subsided and he met my eyes—his hollow and empty—as I lowered my blood-covered muzzle to his throat.

"Stop!"

Stiffening, I kept my focus on the prone warlock rather than turning toward Zander. I wasn't foolish enough to take my eyes off the enemy.

Zander dropped down beside us on his knees, naked, human, and bleeding from a wound on his shoulder. He stared down at the warlock, his lips parted. "He's my mate. I couldn't smell it before. The bond with Trent must have altered his scent, but now it's clear. Don't hurt him. Please."

I dropped my head and growled.

Well, shit.

I allowed the shift to come over me. "Keep him secured. He's dangerous."

Zander nodded, his gaze never wavering from the warlock. "Clay, get the cuffs that are spelled to bind magic."

There was movement behind me. I waited until Zander took my place holding the warlock down, ignoring the hatred that burned in his blue eyes, and then I stood.

"Your Pack Alpha is dead," I said loudly. "Your warlock is defeated. Unless more of you want to die, someone needs to tell us where our omegas are."

A smaller wolf pinned beneath Garrick shifted, squeaking when Garrick's claws sank into his now-exposed skin.

"They're in the basement," he said, baring his throat in submission. "The door over there."

Thank fuck.

I shoved my way to the door. It was locked and warded, but the ward was failing—perhaps in the wake of the warlock's grief. I shoulder-barged it and the door burst open. I caught myself before I fell down the stairs.

"Hello?" a female voice called from below.

"Danny?" I called, taking the stairs two at a time to the bottom. "Are you here?"

Unfortunately, there was no reply, and I could already see that he wasn't.

A dark-skinned woman approached me warily. "I'm Jessie. Danny was here, but they took him away maybe an hour ago."

"No." I slumped. He couldn't be gone. I wouldn't accept it.

"I'm sorry," she whispered. "I don't know where he is."

CHAPTER

# FORTY-SIX

DANNY

Rex parked the car outside a small cabin with corrugated iron cladding and a sloped roof, swearing when the wind buffeted the vehicle.

"Get out," he ordered.

I didn't move. No way in hell was I leaving this car. If I did, Rex would have me one step closer to being locked away inside his cabin prison, and I had the most awful feeling that I'd never leave again.

I wanted to live, and that meant fighting him with everything I had.

Growling with frustration, he got out of the car, slammed his door, and unlocked the back. As he reached inside, I scooted away, doing my best to evade him. Summoning all of my shifter strength, I yanked my wrists apart, snapping the zip tie. He grabbed one of my ankles and dragged me toward the open door.

Gripping the front passenger seat, I held onto it for all I was worth. If only I could partially shift, then I'd be able to sink my claws into it and really dig in, but as it was, my human fingers were useless against Rex's alpha shifter strength.

He yanked me out, pain crashing through me as my knees bashed against the bottom of the doorframe. I landed hard on the snow-covered ground. The wind whipped around us, stinging my cheeks as Rex grabbed the back of my collar and dragged me toward the cabin. I stumbled, my legs so weak from fear that I struggled to keep up with him.

I tripped. The wind captured my cry and carried it away.

That gave me an idea.

Midway between the car and the cabin, I closed my eyes and forced my muscles to go slack.

I dropped to the ground, a deadweight.

Rex paused, perhaps to listen to my pulse to check whether I was faking unconsciousness. Fortunately for me, I doubted he'd be able to tell over the roaring of the wind, which was gathering strength with every passing second.

He huffed, and bent over me. Quick as I could, I whipped up and drove my fist into his balls. He shouted and curled over, covering himself protectively. I scrambled past him, lurched to my feet and sprinted away from him and the cabin.

Ahead of me, twin headlights pierced the gray of dusk. I waved my arms frantically, shouting in the hopes that whoever it was would see me and stop. The car skidded onto the side of the road and the passenger door was thrown open.

Knox stepped out.

A sob caught in my throat and I threw myself into his arms. He pulled me against his broad chest and I buried my face there and breathed him in.

Zander and Everett spilled from the car behind him and

circled around to grab Rex. I clutched Knox, refusing to let him go even as I heard Zander inform Rex of his rights. Bitter coldness stung my cheeks and the sensitive skin beneath my nose.

I was crying, the tears freezing on my skin.

"You're here," I gasped, trying to climb Knox, relieved when he hooked his arms beneath my thighs and hoisted me up so I could wrap my legs around him and cling like a koala. He smelled of sweat and blood, but the salty, metallic combination didn't bother me because I could tell he wasn't injured. The blood wasn't his, or if it was, he'd healed.

"You did good." He nuzzled the side of my neck. "You're safe now, baby. You got away."

My eyes flew open and I looked at him in wonderment. "I did?"

"Yeah." His forehead creased, and his gaze burned into me. "I'm proud of you, and I'm so fucking happy you're okay."

I escaped.

All on my own.

Perhaps Rex would have caught me if my family hadn't shown up or perhaps he wouldn't, but either way, I hadn't rolled over and accepted my fate. I'd fought him, and I'd won.

I wasn't weak, like he'd said.

I was strong.

Not a victim, or a coward, but a strong omega with a loyal and trustworthy mate who'd fought our enemies to find me when I'd been taken from him.

My heart battered against my ribcage, bruised and weary but so full it could burst.

"I love you," I told him.

His eyes lit up, glowing green. "You do?"

I grinned and nodded, but then winced, my head throbbing. "So much."

He kissed me gently, tenderly, drawing back when the wind rocked us. "I love you too. I was so scared when I realized you'd been taken. I'm sorry for not protecting you better. I shouldn't have left your side."

I cupped his face between my hands. "You came for me, just like I knew you would. I just wish…"

"What, baby?" He searched my eyes. "I'll give you anything you want."

I had no doubt that was true.

"When they had me, I wished I had a proper connection to you." I rubbed my chest. "One that I could feel in here, and that they couldn't take away."

His muscles tensed. "You did?"

"Yeah." I nibbled on my lower lip, my heart still going crazy. "Will you mate me tonight?"

His breath stuttered. "Of course, but aren't you scared? I'd understand if you need to wait for a while."

I started to shake my head, then remembered that it was sore. "I've waited for long enough."

He looked torn. "You're injured."

"I'm healing." Already, my back no longer ached. My head still did, but if I shifted, the worst of that would fade.

"Danny?"

Zander walked toward us slowly, caution lining his face. "Rex is in the car. We'll take him straight to the station and keep him under lock and key until he's transferred to another facility. I promise, he won't get near you again."

"Good." I glanced at the car, only now realizing that if I were to get a ride back, I'd either have to drive in Rex's car or in the police cruiser alongside him.

Seeming to recognize my distress, Knox tilted my face

away from the vehicle. "Why don't you and I shift and run home together?"

I stiffened. "They gave me a drug. It stopped me from shifting. And there are other omegas, at a house in Moonlight Cove. We have to help them."

Everett kissed the tip of my nose affectionately. "We've already freed them. We only found you because one of the wolves was willing to talk in exchange for Zander telling his bosses that he'd been cooperative. Before we left, Jessie was able to shift. The drug wears off. She was dosed earlier than you, but with my help, we should be able to guide you through it."

He looked so calm, so sure.

"Can you guys wait until we've figured out if it will work?" I asked Zander.

My brother nodded. "Take your time, Danny. I'll get Everett to drive Rex around the corner so he can't see you."

I closed my eyes and focused on the connection between me and my bear.

*Come on. Wake up.*

# CHAPTER
# FORTY-SEVEN

*NOX*

"Would you prefer to strip or keep your clothes on?" I asked, aware of the bitterly cold wind blowing around us and the blanket of snow on the ground.

He shivered. "Keep them on. But can you help me out if I get stuck?"

"Of course, baby." I'd do anything for him. Didn't he know that by now?

I lowered him to the ground and supported his weight until I was sure he wouldn't fall. Blood plastered the side of his head, and I almost growled. If not for how vulnerable Danny was, I probably would have, but I didn't want to scare him.

Rex was lucky that Zander and Everett had gotten to him while I'd been distracted. If I'd gotten my hands on him, I would have painted the snow with his blood.

I put my hands on Danny's shoulders and gazed into his eyes, allowing my wolf to surface. Gold flickered in Danny's eyes, but his bear was still suppressed. According to the Red Moon Pack's medic, the drug essentially put a shifter's animal side to sleep, but Danny's bear should react to the presence of his mate.

"Show me," I murmured. "Come out, beautiful. Let me see you."

He held my gaze. For a long moment, nothing happened, but then his eyes flashed gold.

"I feel him," he said shakily.

"Hold onto the thread connecting you." I inhaled, scenting him. "Come on, baby. You can do it. Come and play with me."

The gold returned, and Danny's features scrunched.

"Don't try so hard." I kissed him. "Just let it come naturally. As easily as breathing."

He relaxed, and after a few seconds, the change began to roll over him. It took longer than usual. His bones reformed slowly, and I could tell from his expression that it hurt, but he didn't complain. Eventually, the human was gone and he was all bear.

"Good job." My hands twitched. I wanted to bury them in his fur, but until he was healed, I'd have to handle him carefully.

I stripped off my clothes and tossed them to Zander. "I've got it from here."

I shifted and padded over the snow, allowing my nose to guide me home. Danny sidled along with me, moving slowly at first, but gradually picking up speed as his mind started to clear and his aches and pains faded.

By the time we arrived at his place, I was almost shaking from the force of my relief. I shifted and used his spare key to unlock the door. Danny hesitated to shift back, and I paused to wait. I should have considered that he might be anxious about reversing the change, but it hadn't crossed my mind.

"Come on, mate." My fangs lengthened and I bared them at him. "Don't you want me to claim you?"

Immediately, he took a step forward, his fur receding and his body shrinking inward, becoming human.

"That was a dirty tactic," he said once he was able to speak. "Teasing me with your knot and your bite."

I went to him and smoothed his hair back from his face. The cut had knitted itself back together, although it wasn't fully healed.

"Are you sure you want that now?"

He rolled his eyes. "Yes, Knox." His expression softened. "I can feel our connection again. The warlock's magic must have worn off when the drug did."

I glanced at the door. "You wouldn't rather go and visit your mom? I'm sure she's worried about you."

He stalked toward me. "She can wait for a while longer. My brothers will let her know that I'm safe. Right now, I need you."

My cock filled. If my omega needed me, I couldn't leave him unsatisfied.

I made one last effort to be honorable. "We can leave the mating bite until later, when you've calmed down a bit."

Danny's lips pressed together and his eyes narrowed. "Mate. Me. Now."

I gulped. "Okay."

I wasn't stupid enough to deny him. I scooped him up and carried him to his bedroom, greedily dragging gulps of his syrupy sweet scent into my lungs. His skin felt hot against mine, almost feverish, and the heady musk of his arousal made it difficult for me to think.

I placed him gently on the bed and he immediately grabbed his cock and started tugging it. My claws pricked my palms and I clenched my hands, resisting the urge to growl at him that no one was allowed to touch his cock other than me.

He needed me to be gentle. Gentle, and tender, and—

"Hurry up and fuck me." He rolled over, baring his hole. "Please, alpha. I need you."

Oh, fuck.

I grabbed his ass. It was a perky, bouncy peach, full and delicious and already leaking slick.

"Gotta be careful." The words were hard to get out. "Can't hurt you."

He made a sound somewhere between frustration and anguish. "Need your knot, Knox. Fucking need you. Please."

Ah, shit. My omega needed me, and I couldn't let him down. Now wasn't the time for taking it slow. We could enjoy each other properly later. For now, it seemed as if all of the self-control Danny had been exercising for months had finally collapsed and he'd been bowled over by a tsunami of desperate need and desire.

I was happy to be washed away with him.

I knelt on the end of the bed and buried my face in his ass, stiffening my tongue and stabbing his hole with it. He wailed and arched his back, rubbing himself against me. I lapped at him, groaning at the taste of how badly he wanted me.

I worked him open quickly and efficiently. It didn't take long. His body knew what it wanted, even if his mind had taken longer to come around.

"You taste so good." I reached around, knocked his hand off his dick and replaced it with my own. He pulsed in my grip and a shudder ran through him.

"Fill me," he panted. "Stuff me with your cock, alpha. Show me I'm yours."

Every atom in my body vibrated with months of repressed desire as I lined myself up and pushed inside his hole. His channel sucked me in, squeezing around me, hot and tight and...

Gods. This wouldn't even last two minutes.

Danny fisted the bed covers and thrust back, taking me deeper. A litany of pleas spilled from his mouth as I began to move.

I rode him like a beast.

It wasn't soft or easy, as I'd intended. It was passionate, almost feral, driven by our most basic instincts. I pounded into his spot with every thrust and kept a hold of his cock, pumping it in the same rhythm.

He moaned louder, and my chest puffed out. My wolf was pleased that we were satisfying our mate.

Finally, Danny screamed and shot all over the bed. His ass clenched around me, forcing my orgasm. I roared as I poured into him, and I latched my teeth onto his shoulder and bit, the coppery tang of his blood filling my mouth.

His cock twitched, emptying more cum onto the bed, and he reared back onto his knees and twisted toward me. Our eyes locked and he bared his fangs, then sank them into the crook of my shoulder.

I hardly noticed the brief sting of pain, too entranced by the way his presence wrapped around me like a comforting blanket. Foreign emotions flickered through me. Disbelief, wonderment, joy.

He retracted his fangs and licked the wound. I did the same to his, watching it heal before my eyes, leaving a pink mark that would show anyone who cared to look that he was mine.

*Mine, mine, mine.*

My eyes widened. Those hadn't been my thoughts, but his.

Carefully, I maneuvered us onto our sides and wrapped my arms around him, my cock still deep inside him. I closed my eyes and sensed his bear twining around my wolf, both animal sides ecstatic about their new connection.

*Mate.*

*Ours.*

*Protect.*

*Love.*

"I love you," I whispered out loud, so he'd know that the human part of me cared for him as deeply as the wolf did.

"I love you too," he murmured, his voice sleepy and sated.

I nuzzled the back of his neck, running my nose over the mating mark. "How long do you think we have before your family turns up?"

# FORTY-EIGHT

*D*ANNY

Just as we got out of the shower, there was a knock at the front door. I groaned. Even without my shifter senses, I knew that my family would be clustered on the doorstep, waiting to see us.

More than anything, I wanted to climb straight into bed with Knox for another round, but I couldn't just ignore them. They deserved better than me thinking with my dick.

"I can send them away if you need more time," Knox said, taking the towel from the rail and drying me so tenderly that it brought tears to my eyes.

"No, I want to see them. I'm just a little overwhelmed by everything that's happened and part of me wants to hide from the world."

Knox kissed my cheek. "If you want to hide, I'll build you a pillow fort when they're gone. What do you say?"

I melted into his arms. "That sounds pretty perfect."

He kissed me again, but then pulled away and brushed the towel over the skin that had been dampened when I touched him.

"I'll get the door." He tugged on a pair of sweatpants

and a T-shirt, the fabric plastering itself to his skin since he hadn't bothered to dry himself, only me. "You finish getting dressed."

He waited for me to nod before leaving the bathroom. I ignored the sound of him moving through the house, glad for a moment of peace. I dried my hair properly and dressed in a pair of full-length pajamas and fluffy socks. Perhaps I didn't strictly need them in order to keep warm, but there was something comforting about soft fabric against my skin.

With nothing else to distract me, I headed to the living area. As soon as I entered, Momma flew around the room and pulled me into a rib-crushing hug.

"My baby!" she cried. "You're okay!"

"I told you he was," Everett muttered from somewhere behind her. I couldn't see him. I was too busy trying to breathe. Sometimes, Momma forgot how strong she was.

She rocked me from side to side, sniffling in my ear and clutching me as though she was afraid to let go. Guilt lanced through me. I should have gone to see her earlier rather than falling into bed with Knox. I'd been stressed and not thinking clearly. While I didn't regret what we'd done, I felt bad for not reassuring her sooner.

She drew back, blinking rapidly to restrain the tears gleaming in her eyes. "Is that a mating bite?"

I cocked my head, surprised. I'd expected an admonishment for scaring her, or perhaps concern over what had happened.

"It is!" The sides of her mouth hooked up and her eyes sparkled. She spun toward Knox, her gaze narrowing in on the spot beneath his T-shirt where the puncture marks were. He pulled it aside so she could see, and she squeaked. "Oh, my baby. You're mated! I'm so happy for you."

"I think it's clear who the favorite child is," Garrick teased.

Momma smoothed her hands down the front of my pajamas and tutted. "I'm allowed to be excited for my youngest son. Our only omega." Her eyes welled again. "I was so…"

"Shh, Momma. It's okay." I hugged her, startled as another pair of arms wrapped around us. I breathed in cherries and vanilla. Milo. "I'm safe."

"You'd better be." Milo squeezed tighter. "Don't ever scare me like that again."

A growl rumbled from Everett. "Everyone is going to be careful from now on. No one will worry my pregnant mate. Got it?"

I laughed. "Got it, Ev."

He might not have said the words, but in his own way, he'd voiced his concern for me.

"Son."

Milo and Momma released me and stepped aside to give Dad space to approach. He cupped the back of my head, scenting me, and then enveloped me in his arms, his chest vibrating as he held me close and smothered me with feelings of *safe-clan-home*.

"Is everyone all right?" I asked him, finally realizing that I didn't know exactly what had gone on earlier and whether we'd emerged unscathed.

He let me out of the hug but slid his arm around my shoulders to keep me close. No doubt his Clan Alpha instincts were insisting he stay close until he was certain I'd be fine.

"We had a few injuries." His expression was serious. "Nothing major. Dr. Black had to patch up a couple of people, but they'll heal quickly.

"No…" I swallowed. "No fatalities?"

"Not on our side. They lost their alpha and a couple of others."

I frowned. Someone was missing. "Where's Zander?"

Dad stiffened. "He's at the police station, making sure our omegas are healed and questioned before they're sent home. We also found five other omegas on the premises who were being kept as slaves. Dr. Black is seeing to them, but they've suffered extensive trauma. Even if their bodies heal, their minds might never be the same."

My stomach twisted. Gods, I hadn't even considered that there might be others like us, either taken from other clans or belonging to the families within the rogue pack.

"Those poor people." I couldn't imagine what they must have been through. Didn't want to, if I was honest. "I'm sorry I didn't come to the station to help. Maybe I could have—"

Dad cut me off with a look. "No one is angry with you. We're glad you had Knox to bring you home and take care of you. There's no reason for you to feel guilty. You can visit with the other omegas tomorrow or later this week if you'd like. We'll be trying to track down their relatives, but that might not be possible for all of them."

Because the rogue wolf pack might have decimated their families. Those poor, poor people.

"Jamie?" I asked. "Jessie and Hannah?"

"They're all okay," Dad said. "None of them were harmed beyond the original abduction."

"And Jamie's mom?"

"She's fine. They weren't interested in her. Hamish is looking after her at the Omega House until Jamie has recovered enough to take over her care again."

"Thank gods." I squeezed Dad, then broke away from him and went straight to Knox, looping my arms around him and burying my face in his chest.

All was quiet.

Too quiet.

My scalp prickled. "What is it? Something else is going on too."

Momma's hand ran down my back. "Nothing you need to worry about right now."

Huffing, I turned in Knox's arms and glared at her. "Tell me."

She exchanged a glance with Dad, but it was Garrick who spoke.

"Did you meet a warlock while you were at the Pack House?" he asked.

"No." I'd known they must have one, but I hadn't seen a trace of them.

He nodded, his body unusually tense. "His name is Reid. He was mated to their Alpha."

"I—"

"That bastard forced a mating upon him." Garrick's fists clenched, and he sounded more furious than I'd ever heard him.

I felt sick. "He… he mated the warlock against his will?"

Reid. His name was Reid. For some reason, I couldn't bring myself to use it. The idea of forcing someone into an unwanted bond was horrific. Mate bonds were supposed to bring reassurance and create emotional closeness with a partner, but as with all things, they had a dark side. They could be used to control. To remove free will.

Even worse, the warlock—Reid—would still feel the pain of the loss as if it were a mate he'd chosen.

"Reid has been inconsolable," Dad said quietly. "He hasn't spoken to us himself, but some of the others have. The woman they've designated as their spokesperson said that Reid was picked up in a town they passed through several months ago, and the Pack Alpha mated him so he could control his magic.”

My chest ached and my eyes burned. “That’s awful.”

“And now he’s grieving the bastard,” Garrick growled. “Meanwhile, his true mate can’t do anything to help him.”

“His true mate?” This just got worse. Had the pack torn him from a mate to force the abomination of a bond between him and their Pack Alpha?

“Zander,” Momma whispered, her face creased with pain.

“Oh.” My heart sank. “Oh, no.”

“But enough of that,” Momma said briskly, swiping at her eyes. “The good news is that Rex is locked up and he’ll be transported out of Grizzly Ridge tomorrow. He’s going to a magically enhanced prison for a long time and he’ll never get anywhere near you ever again.”

“Especially not if he has an ‘accident’ in prison,” Knox grumbled under his breath.

No one chastened him.

“Good riddance.” The sooner I could forget the man, the better. “I want to visit the omegas tomorrow. All of them, including Reid.”

Knox’s lips brushed over my temple. “We’ll make it happen.”

CHAPTER

# FORTY-NINE

**K** *NOX*

"Why are you so nervous?" Danny asked as we walked down the street toward his parents' house the following Sunday. "We've done this before. You already know my family. There's nothing to worry about."

He could say that all he wanted, but it didn't stop the ball of anxiety from tangling tighter in my gut. Sure, I'd been around his family before, but always as a *prospective* mate. We were actually mated now. It was done. Would that change things?

"Is it because you were exiled from your pack?" Danny slipped his hand into mine. "No one cares. I doubt they even know. I promise, it won't be like that here. You'll always be welcome."

Gods, I hoped he was right. This was the closest I'd come to feeling like I belonged in a long, long time.

Danny didn't bother to knock. He opened the door and bowled straight inside. My mouth watered as the scents of cooked meat and roasted vegetables greeted us.

"In here," Melinda called from the formal dining room.

We followed her voice and she met us in the doorway.

265

She hugged Danny, and then me. As soon as her arms closed around me, I froze. My heart hammered, and I didn't know what to do. How long had it been since someone had held me in a warm, motherly embrace?

I loved being close to my mate, but it was very different from the comfort of hugging a parent.

She patted my back. "Come and sit down, my boys. The food is already on the table." She gave us a knowing look. "I'm not surprised you're the last ones to get here. The newly mated are often like that."

My cheeks heated and I looked down at my hands. Danny snorted. Melinda tittered. I pretended I hadn't had Danny on my knot just half an hour ago.

The dining room was toasty, and the overhead lights were partially dimmed but bright enough to see what we needed to. Aaron was seated at the far end of the table with an empty chair beside him. The half-drunk wine glass told me that it was Melinda's seat. The men in the family seemed to prefer beer. Or whiskey.

Garrick sat opposite Melinda, with Zander beside him. The sheriff looked worn out, with dark shadows beneath his eyes, suggesting he hadn't slept well since the raid on the Red Moon Pack.

I didn't blame him. From what I'd heard, his mate had refused to engage with anyone. The warlock didn't speak, hardly ate, and just sat in Dr. Black's warded back room, crying for hours on end. That had to weigh on Zander.

Milo beamed at Danny from the spot beside Melinda, who sat and sipped her wine, and Everett loomed like a protective wall on Milo's other side. Danny dropped into the chair beside Zander and I claimed the one beside him. No one sat opposite me, but perhaps that was for the best. It meant less pressure.

Less opportunity for them to surround me and interrogate me.

But as the conversation began, it was light. Friendly. I started to relax.

"Help yourselves," Melinda said, lifting the cover off a pot of stew.

My breath hitched, and I stared, then sniffed. It was venison stew. Perhaps it was a coincidence, but as the family uncovered the rest of the dishes, and I spotted both rare steak and macaroni and cheese among the offerings, I knew it couldn't be.

Emotion clogged my throat, and I struggled to breathe past it. Tears welled in my eyes and threatened to spill down my cheeks.

"Knox!" Melinda exclaimed, alarmed. "Are you okay?"

I rubbed my chest, unsure of the answer.

Was I okay?

I was part of a new clan. I had a mate, and that mate's family had gone out of their way to prepare some of my favorite dishes on the first night we shared a meal after the mating.

"I... I..."

"Did we get it wrong?" Worry laced Milo's tone.

"No." I sniffed. *Get yourself under control.* I met Milo's eyes, and then Melinda's. No doubt they were responsible for this. "Thank you so much."

Melinda offered a small smile. "We wanted you to feel welcome."

"I do." I coughed to clear my throat. "I'm, uh, touched."

I had a feeling my cheeks were even redder than before.

"The pack Knox grew up in wasn't like ours," Danny said, reaching under the table to lay his hand on my thigh.

One side of my mouth hitched up. "That's an understatement. They were old school. My mom was great, but other than her, no one showed much affection or went out of their way for anyone else. It's just... really nice of you to do this."

"Of course." Melinda's hand twitched, as if she wanted to reach for me. "You're family now."

"That means a lot to me." I didn't bother hiding the emotion in my voice.

Danny grabbed the macaroni and cheese and dragged it over, scooping a large portion onto my plate. That broke the ice, and everyone went for the food, even little Milo, who seemed to have learned how strong a shifter's appetite could be and how quick he needed to be to get whatever food he wanted.

Not that I thought Everett would ever let him go hungry. Just like I wouldn't let Danny go hungry. We were mates. And this...

This was a family.

For the first time, I felt like part of it.

I stared at each of them in turn, a grin stretching my face. It wasn't just *a* family, but *my* family.

"What?" Danny asked, nudging me with his shoulder.

"Nothing." I leaned over to nuzzle him. "Pass the steak."

# EPILOGUE –
# VALENTINE'S DAY

K*NOX*

I wandered home more slowly than usual, aware that once I arrived, I'd have to figure out how to break the news to Danny that he was pregnant.

It wasn't fair of me to sit on the knowledge without informing him. My nose was far more sensitive than his, and as far as I could tell, other than a slight alteration to his scent, he wasn't experiencing any other symptoms.

It didn't seem right for me to tell him what was going on in his own body, but I couldn't pretend not to know either. There was no way I could hide my excitement. He'd be able to tell I was hiding something, and he'd be angry when he learned the truth.

I had to do it.

I passed Aaron and Melinda's house and raised my hand to Melinda, who was visible through the front window. She waved back.

Besides, it wasn't as if this was bad news. We were mated. Our little pup or cub was growing inside him. He'd be thrilled. But I had no idea how to tell him.

Perhaps I should take him out to dinner. There weren't

any nice restaurants in town, but we could go to the diner or I could try my hand at making the meal myself, although I wasn't about to win any prizes for my cooking.

It needed to be special.

The sun, which was already low on the horizon, slipped behind a cloud, and I shivered as the air temperature dipped. I arrived at the path to Danny's house—our house—and drew in a deep breath. The faint scent of steak and vegetables greeted me. Danny must have already cooked for us. There would be no romantic dinner out tonight.

My gut twisting with a combination of apprehension and excitement, I headed to the front door, unlocked it, and let myself in. I followed the smell of food to the kitchen. It was empty, but Danny had dinner already served on the dining table, along with a tall, foamy glass of beer, condensation beading on the outside.

"What's this?" I asked, arching my eyebrow at my mate, who was hovering behind the dining table, looking gorgeous in dark jeans and a pink button-up shirt.

"Our Valentine's dinner." He smiled, but his heart rate was elevated and the salty scent of his sweat would have been obvious to any shifter.

I rounded the table, drew him into my arms, and kissed him. "Smells delicious. But what's going on, baby? Why are you nervous?"

He relaxed against my chest, melting into me in the way I so loved. He turned his face into the side of my neck and breathed me in, nuzzling the mating mark on my shoulder.

Finally, he drew back, his pulse steadier. He reached into his back pocket and drew something out. He passed it to me, and I stared.

A knitted bootie, with something poking out of it.

A pregnancy test.

One with two lines in the center.

My gaze flew to his. He knew.

Danny's lower lip wobbled. "We're going to be dads."

Grinning, I wrapped my arms around him and squeezed. "Thank gods."

He pushed at me. "What do you mean, 'Thank gods'?"

I brushed his hair back from his face and kissed him, savoring the softness of his lips against mine. "I could smell it, but I didn't know how to tell you. I was going to say something tonight, but I wasn't sure how you'd react to me telling you about what was going on inside you, since you should have been the first one to know."

Danny looped his arms around my neck and smiled at me warmly. "You silly wolf. You can't help what you smell. Are you happy?"

My chest expanded with pride. "Beyond happy. This is amazing news. Having you is more than I ever imagined. You and a little one… that's the stuff dreams are made of."

"Good." He pressed closer, his still-flat belly plastered to my abs. "Because I couldn't be more pleased to make a family with you."

*Family.*

I closed my eyes, touched my lips to his temple, and let the word soak in.

I'd found a home here with him in Grizzly Ridge, and I'd considered myself the luckiest bastard alive because of it.

But now, I'd have a family with him.

A family of my own.

A rumble of pleasure rippled through me. "I love you."

Danny snuggled into the embrace. "I love you too, mate. Always."

THE END

# ABOUT THE AUTHOR

A.J. Cane writes LGBTQIA+ paranormal romance with love interests who will make you swoon. A.J. can usually be found reading, writing, or eating way too much chocolate.